FATHOM FIVE

FATHOM FIVE

THE UNWRITTEN BOOKS

FATHOM FIVE

by James Bow

A BOARDWALK BOOK
A MEMBER OF THE DUNDURN GROUP
TORONTO

Editor: Barry Jowett   Design: Alison Carr
Printer: Webcom

Library and Archives Canada Cataloguing in Publication

Bow, James, 1972-
      Fathom five / James Bow.

Sequel to: The unwritten girl.
ISBN 978-1-55002-692-4

      I. Title.

PS8603.O973F48 2007   jC813'.6   C2007-900859-3

1   2   3   4   5   11   10   09   08   07

We acknowledge the support of the **Canada Council for the Arts** and the **Ontario Arts Council** for our publishing program. We also acknowledge the financial support of the **Government of Canada** through the **Book Publishing Industry Development Program** and **The Association for the Export of Canadian Books**, and the **Government of Ontario** through the **Ontario Book Publishers Tax Credit program** and the **Ontario Media Development Corporation**.

Care has been taken to trace the ownership of copyright material used in this book. The author and the publisher welcome any information enabling them to rectify any refer-ences or credits in subsequent editions.

J. Kirk Howard, President

Printed and bound in Canada
Printed on recycled paper
www.dundurn.com

The author gratefully acknowledges the Ontario Arts Council for assistance with this project through the Writers' Reserve Program.

Dundurn Press	Gazelle Book Services Limited	Dundurn Press
3 Church Street, Suite 500	White Cross Mills	2250 Military Road
Toronto, Ontario, Canada	High Town, Lancaster, England	Tonawanda, NY
M5E 1M2	LA1 4XS	U.S.A. 14150

For Vivian

ARIEL:
Come unto these yellow sands,
And then take hands:
Courtsied when you have and kiss'd
The wild waves whist,
Foot it featly here and there;
And, sweet sprites, the burthen bear.
Hark, hark!

FERDINAND:
Where should this music be? i' the air or the earth?
It sounds no more: and sure, it waits upon
Some god o' the island. Sitting on a bank,
Weeping again the king my father's wreck,
This music crept by me upon the waters,
Allaying both their fury and my passion
With its sweet air: thence I have follow'd it,
Or it hath drawn me rather. But 'tis gone.
No, it begins again.

ARIEL *sings.*
Full fathom five thy father lies;
Of his bones are coral made;
Those are pearls that were his eyes:
Nothing of him that doth fade
But doth suffer a sea-change
Into something rich and strange.
Sea-nymphs hourly ring his knell

— William Shakespeare: *The Tempest*

CHAPTER ONE
IT BEGINS AGAIN

"Peter! Storm's coming!"

It was a beautiful day. Peter slid across the ice in the wading pool in the middle of the deserted park. The sun shone through the frozen willow tree. Ice coated its branches and it clicked like a wooden wind chime as it shifted in the breeze.

Fiona sat shivering on the bench. She pointed to a towering purple cloud approaching from the northwest.

"Come on, Peter; storm's coming. Probably more freezing rain, so let's go home."

Peter slid up to her, beaming. "But it's still sunny *here.*"

"Not for long," said Fiona. She reached out. "Come home, now."

The nine-year-old took his babysitter's hand.

Together, they walked along the crusty snow, avoiding the smooth and slippery asphalt path.

As they approached the street, Fiona looked up. "Your parents are home!"

Peter saw his parents climbing down from a streetcar. Dad took Mom's arm as he helped her to the curb.

A horn blared. A pickup truck slid forward, its wheels locked. His father looked up.

There was a sickening thump.

Fiona screamed and ran, skidding and slipping on the ice.

Peter fell on the ice-hardened asphalt. A pain shot up his arm.

In the distance, sirens wailed.

***

Peter's eyes snapped open. The light of an October morning seeped past his blinds and into his bedroom. His sheets were twisted around him. His cheeks were wet.

He touched his face, and stared at the moisture on his fingertips as if he had never seen it before.

His clock radio switched on with a babble of voices. He groaned and whacked it silent.

The house was quiet and cold. He frowned at the silence before remembering that he was the only one at home. His uncle was off to Chicago on business, and wouldn't be back until early next week, just in time to celebrate Peter's sixteenth birthday.

Peter threw on jeans and a Maple Leafs' t-shirt over a long-sleeved shirt and tried to make his hair look less like a haystack. What *had* he been doing in his sleep, skydiving? He only remembered falling. He tossed the comforter over the knotted sheets and went galumphing down to breakfast.

He was scraping the hard butter over a rapidly disintegrating slice of toast when the school bus horn blared outside. He shoved the toast into his mouth, grabbed his battered school bag and his windbreaker, and sprinted down his walkway just in time.

Some of his fellow students called his name as he walked down the aisle of the bus. He nodded at them and sat in an empty seat near the back, staring out the window and trying to swallow the lump of toast.

A moment later, the bus stopped again. The door opened, and a cardboard box on legs wobbled up the aisle and stopped beside Peter. Suddenly, the box lunged at him and bonked him in the nose. He grappled with it as Rosemary swung off her backpack and dropped into the seat beside him. She was wearing jeans and a bulky grey cardigan sweater. "Thanks," she said. "I'll take it back, now."

His mouth glued shut by toast, Peter did his best to say, "That's okay, I've got it," with his eyebrows. He didn't think he was successful, because she answered, "Science project. You know, those electron shell balloon models we were working on on Saturday? It's not heavy, but it's kind of awkward."

She slid the box onto her lap, glanced at him again, and pushed her glasses further up on her nose. "Are you *still* eating breakfast?" The quirk on her lips was a dare for him to laugh.

With a mighty effort, he swallowed. "Nope."

"You know, Peter, if you'd just set your clock radio to go off five minutes earlier —"

Peter laughed. "You say that every day. It's not going to happen."

Rosemary snorted. Then she frowned at him. "You look tired."

Peter caught himself in a yawn. Last night had not been good, but he couldn't remember why. "Funny dream or something," he said after a while.

"Not worried about your French mid-term, are you?" Rosemary gave him a teasing smile.

Peter stared at her, his stomach leaden with toast. He had forgotten to study for his French mid-term last night.

***

When Peter next saw Rosemary, after the school bells summoned them from first period, she was pulling books from her locker amidst the torrent of students rushing between classes. She had her textbooks around her in neat piles, and was sorting through them for the one she had misplaced. Her face lit up when she saw Peter. "How did the French test go?"

Peter's smile vanished. He began thumping his head on the nearest locker. "Oh, God! How do you say 'I'm going to kill myself' in French?"

"Um ... *Je vais me tuer*, I think. Was it really that bad?"

"I'll be lucky if I get a 'B'!"

"Oh, a 'B'! You'll be lucky if you don't die of shame!"

He drooped. "I'm just glad it's over."

Rosemary smiled sympathetically. She touched his shoulder, and there they stayed a moment. The background chatter seemed to soften.

Then Benson barged in and opened his locker with a clatter, sending Peter and Rosemary scrambling apart. "Hey there!" he exclaimed. "How are the lovebirds today?"

Rosemary reddened and Peter flared. "We're not lovebirds!" said the two in unison.

"Yeah, yeah," said Benson's friend, Joe, as he stepped up to his locker. He stopped and nudged Peter's school bag with his foot. "Pete, isn't this bag new? What do you do, play soccer with this thing?"

Peter sucked his teeth and said nothing.

Benson's voice came from deep within his locker. "Either of you figure out question four from our history assignment? Stumped me."

"Benson!" Rosemary exclaimed. "The War of 1812 ended in 1814!"

"Yeah?" Benson closed his locker. "Then why do they just call it the War of 1812? Doesn't make sense, does it? History never makes sense. Speaking of, you folks ready for your history presentation? I've got the coolest!"

"I'm not presenting till Wednesday," said Rosemary.

But Benson turned away. He focussed on a girl with golden curls who'd opened a locker beside them. He grinned, slicked back his hair, and stepped forward. "Hey, Veronica!"

Veronica gave him a glance, then buried her face in the locker. "Hey, Benson."

Benson sucked in his breath. "You want to go to the Halloween Homecoming Dance?"

Veronica lit up. "Oh! I'd love to!" She turned back to shelving her textbooks.

Benson beamed. But as Veronica continued to focus on her locker, uncertainty crept across his face. "Um ... so, when do I pick you up?"

She looked at him. "What?" Then her mouth twitched in mock sympathy. "Oh! You meant with *you*, didn't you?" She closed her locker and strode away.

Joe patted Benson's shoulder. "Ouch."

"Oooo," Rosemary winced. "Bet she's going as the Ice Queen."

Despite himself, Peter snorted. "Yeah, cold. You walked right into that one, B."

Benson scowled at him. "I haven't seen you try to invite anybody."

Peter suddenly found himself staring at Rosemary. Rosemary looked back at him. Her brow furrowed. They stood a long moment, blinking at each other. Peter felt his cheeks redden. "Well, I —"

But Benson turned back to his locker. "So, what are you presenting, Pete? You're up after me."

Peter stopped cold. The leaden feeling in his stomach returned. History homework. That was the other thing he had forgotten. What *had* he been doing last night?

"*Falling*," answered a small, lost voice.

He flicked his hand past his ear and looked over his shoulder, but no one was there.

★★★

Peter stepped out onto the porch of Rosemary's house. The sky was a deep blue, with the moon rising over the trees. Rosemary stepped out after him.

"Thanks," he said. "Your father's a good cook."

Rosemary smirked. "He can teach you, you know. Then you won't have to rely on pot noodle when you're home alone."

"Well, maybe someday," he shrugged. "How's your brother doing?"

She rolled her eyes. "Still fretting over which graduate school to go to, poor Theo. He's thinking about literary criticism at McGill."

"I'm sure he'll pick something good." He grinned at her. "Thanks for the homework help, too."

Rosemary touched his shoulder. "You're welcome."

The front door opened again and Mr. Watson peered out. "Still here, Peter?"

Peter and Rosemary split apart, taking great interest in the posts and the cracked walk.

Mr. Watson smiled. "You're sure you don't want a ride home?"

Peter shuffled on the concrete steps. "I'm sure. It's only a mile, and it's a nice night."

"See you at school tomorrow," said Rosemary, starting towards him but bringing herself up short. Mr. Watson was still in the doorway.

"Yeah," said Peter. "See you." He turned away, trudging down the front walk and along the gravel shoulder of the road, cursing himself for being so tongue-tied around Rosemary's father.

Why do I feel like I'm under a microscope when

he's around? he thought. It's not as if I'm Rosemary's future husband.

He lingered over that image a moment, then shook it out of his head.

Rosemary would die laughing if she heard that. Or kill me.

The road on which he and Rosemary lived was lined with trees for half a mile between their homes. Emerging from a tunnel of leaves, he was hit by a sharp wind blowing across an open field. The trees behind him shook with a sound like surf.

He pulled his windbreaker closer to his throat and whistled a tune. It was lost in the rush of wind around him. Clouds scudded in front of the moon.

Maybe a storm's coming in, he thought. Maybe there's a Small Craft Advisory on Georgian Bay. Gales across the bay can push small boats against the rocks just like one of those ... what were they called? Water witches? Sirens?

Peter's lips went dry, and he stopped whistling. He pressed on towards his house, kicking up the gravel along the shoulder of the road. He jumped when an owl hooted nearby.

He laughed at himself. Wrong setting. Sirens could hardly tempt *him* to crash his ship against the rocks on 45th Parallel Road. He was on dry land. He wasn't even in a car. Perhaps sirens could entice unwary drivers into ditches, but people walking? That would be an interesting twist on the old legends.

He pressed on past the hissing leaves, until something on the side of the road stopped him in his tracks.

A stone fence ending in a tall gate pushed out along the property line. A shape was perched on top of the gatepost, just a silhouette in the moonlight. The hairs on the back of Peter's neck rose. He was sure that the shape was looking at him.

Obvious explanation, said Peter's rational mind. It's a garden gnome.

Too big.

Maybe the Hendersons put in stone lions.

It doesn't look like a stone lion.

And stone lions don't move.

Peter stood stock-still. The wind rose again, whipping the branches into waves. He began to hear whispers off the leaves and wind. A woman reclined on the brick-and-concrete gatepost in front of him, her arms and legs too long to be human and her hair long enough to cover her like a shroud. Her gaze pinned him until the moon emerged from behind clouds. Pale light shone with such intensity that the telephone poles cast shadows. Peter blinked, and looked at the gate again. There was nothing there.

See? Nothing to worry about.

Peter crunched down the shoulder of the road and

up to his front door as fast as he could walk. He burst into his house, slammed the door behind him, and leaned against it, breathing heavily, wondering why he should feel so scared.

Then he wondered why he should feel so safe.

He had been alone with his thoughts out there, with nothing but the wind to interrupt them. His imagination had gone off on a wild tangent. In his uncle's house, this hadn't changed. The place was dark and empty. His imagination prickled like the hairs on the back of his neck.

Peter turned on every light he passed as he paced through the house, using the bathroom, changing out of his school clothes, and then fixing a snack to eat in front of the television.

The television squawked and babbled. He cycled through the channels with the remote twice, then set it aside with a sigh. After a moment he picked up the phone and dialled.

"Watson residence," answered Rosemary's voice.

"Hey, Rosemary."

"Peter! You only just left here! Dad's going to tease me again!"

He winced. "Sorry."

"Don't worry, I'm used to it. What's up?"

Peter hesitated. This was Rosemary he was talking to, his best friend. But he was still ashamed to say that he had spooked himself in the night and needed a human voice to tell him he wasn't alone.

"Peter, are you okay?"

"Yeah," said Peter abruptly. "Yes. I just needed to hear a friendly voice, that's all."

Rosemary laughed, and they settled down to talk.

* * *

Outside Peter's house, a wisp of light flitted from window to window, before settling upon the kitchen. Inside, past the pile of dirty dishes stacked in the sink before the window, Peter could be seen across the room, talking on the phone and laughing.

The wisp hovered by the window for a moment before vanishing into the night.

CHAPTER TWO
THE SEA-CHANGE

A horn blared. His father looked up. There was a sickening thump.

Fiona screamed and ran for the street. Peter fell on the ice-hardened asphalt. A pain shot up his arm.

People were stepping out of their homes, looking on in horror. The streetcar driver had taken command of the scene, ordering people to call an ambulance. The driver of the pickup truck stood at the curb, his arms around himself, and he was quaking.

Peter held his broken arm and began to cry. In the distance, sirens wailed.

"Come home, Peter."

Peter started. Fiona was beside him, extending her hand.

"Come home."

Something shocked through him like cold water.

Peter's eyes snapped open. He sat up in bed.

* * *

Peter staggered back as the basketball sailed into his hands.

"Heads up, Pete!" shouted Joe, his team captain. "Where's your mind been all day?"

"Huh?" Peter shook the fog from his mind.

"And the prosecution rests, your honour!" Benson snatched the ball from Peter's hands.

"Good practice, boys!" Coach Beckett shouted over the smack of basketballs and the squeak of sneakers. "Group into threes and let's finish with games of keep-away. Then hit the showers."

Joe and Benson each clapped one of Peter's shoulders and marched him to the centre of the gymnasium. Benson bounced the basketball once and tossed it up over Peter's head.

"So ...." Joe snatched the pass and hoisted the ball out of Peter's reach. "Who are you taking to the Halloween Homecoming Dance?"

Peter stopped short. "Nobody."

"What?" asked Benson. "You're going all by your lonesome?"

"I'm not going," Peter huffed as the ball bounced past him.

"Why don't you take your girlfriend?" called Joe.

Peter half-turned, and Benson bounced the ball through his legs. "Hey!"

"Where is Rosemary, anyway?" asked Benson as Peter darted in front of Joe. "She's usually in the stands on Tuesdays."

Peter batted the ball out of the air and caught it. He nodded Joe into the centre. "She couldn't stay. She had stuff to do."

"Too bad," said Joe. He darted into Peter's space, reaching for the ball. "Why don't you ask Rosemary to the dance? It would be a nice treat for her. You have the pick of the girls from Grade 11 on down; she'll be lucky if anyone takes her."

"That's not true!"

"Someone's defending her honour!" sang Benson. He grunted as Peter fired the ball like a bullet.

"Good arm, Peter!" shouted Mr. Beckett from across the gym. "That's the spirit!"

The gym squeaked and banged around them. Benson tossed to Peter. Peter threw the ball back, but Joe knocked it down and motioned Peter back to the centre.

"Look," said Joe as he tossed the ball past Peter, "you could do a lot worse, you know." He caught Benson's pass lightly. "So she's a little short, but you could call her fun-sized — whoa!" He scrambled back as Peter lunged for him.

23

"Good defence, Peter!" the coach called. "Don't take a foul, though!"

Joe covered the ball, twisted, and shot past Peter. Then he held up his hands for forgiveness. "Seriously, you two have been joined at the hip for years."

Benson laughed. "Yeah, so why not dance? She knows how, you know. She took step-dancing classes."

"Yeah," Joe chuckled. "We never let her hear the end of it. Well, we did, but not for a long time."

Peter glared. "She doesn't want to go."

"Did you ask her?" asked Joe.

Peter kept a mutinous silence.

Benson laughed. "He reads her mind, he knows her so well."

"Leave me alone!" Peter snapped. "It's my life, okay?"

"That's big city talk, Pete. Here in Clarksbury, it's everybody's life." Joe grinned shamelessly.

Benson grabbed the ball and stepped closer to Peter, his expression serious for once. "You know, the only reason you two are being teased is because you're both so totally blind. Do you know your free-throw average drops twenty percent whenever she's around?"

"It does not!" Peter yelled. Then he faltered. "Twenty percent?"

"Not twenty, exactly," Joe said, closing in behind

him. "But you did fall over that first day she called to you from the stands."

"Something tripped me!"

Benson snorted. "Yeah. Your feet."

Joe stepped around Peter and stood beside Benson. "Okay, so you say you don't think of Rosemary as more than just a friend? Prove it! Repeat after me: Rosemary and I are just friends."

Peter rolled his eyes. "Rosemary and I are just friends."

"Rosemary and I have *always* been just friends," added Benson.

"Rosemary and I have always been just friends."

Joe's grin was a challenge. "I have absolutely no interest in Rosemary being anything more than just my friend."

"I have no, I have absolutely ...." The words dried in Peter's throat. Joe's and Benson's grins widened.

Joe slapped the basketball into Peter's chest. "Ask her out, you idiot. What's the worst thing that could happen?"

"Well ...." Benson clapped Peter's shoulder. "She could rip out your still-beating heart and crush it under her heel as she walks away."

Joe shrugged. "Yeah, but at least then he'd know."

A sharp whistle cut across the gym. "Okay, boys," shouted the coach, "we're done here. Good practice! Hit the showers!"

Joe and Benson jogged to the change rooms, leaving Peter standing in the centre of the emptying gymnasium, thoughtfully bouncing the basketball.

***

"I'm home!" Peter tossed his coat into the closet. Then he remembered. He stood in the front foyer, listening, but the house said nothing.

He sighed and stepped into the kitchen. He saw the light blinking on the answering machine and he pressed the playback button.

Beep! "Peter, it's Michael. Listen, it looks like they're going to need me to stay another week here in Chicago. Sorry about your birthday — I'll make it up to you when I get home. You, uh, have the number of my hotel, so call if you need anything. You know where my bankcard is. Sorry again, Pete. Love."

The machine clicked off. Peter stared at it a long moment. Then he turned. His eyes fell on his battered school bag: a gift from his uncle for the start of school year, presented fully stocked with school supplies along with a note the morning after his uncle had left for New York.

Peter kicked it down the hall. It sailed into the front door with a satisfying explosion of pens, pencils, and paper.

The house made no sound, not even the creaks of settling that he'd remembered from the townhouse in Toronto.

He picked up the phone and dialled. "Rosemary? You eaten yet? Want to grab a pizza?"

* * *

Rosemary's father drove Peter and Rosemary into town.

"I don't mean to impose," said Peter from the backseat. "I can't wait until I have a driver's licence."

"It's no imposition at all." Mr. Watson grinned. "Indeed, it gives us a chance to chat. How have you been, Peter?"

"Um, fine," said Peter. He shot a "save me" look at Rosemary, but she didn't.

"How are things at school?"

"Uh ... good!"

"How's your uncle? In good form, is he?"

"Yes. He is."

"So, when can I expect Rosemary back from this hot date?"

"Bluh," said Peter.

"Dad!" Rosemary cuffed her father on the shoulder. "We'll call for a ride before ten, okay?"

Peter stared out the car window. Night was falling earlier every day, and the lights were already on, washing a sickly orange glow over the road's rocky embankments.

The shadows flickered as they passed, like frames of a moving picture. Peter thought he could make out a lithe figure running along the rock wall, keeping pace with the car, but when he looked closer, there was nothing there.

A few minutes later, the car pulled up in front of a restaurant in the middle of Clarksbury's downtown strip. The sign above the door read *Luigi's Pizzeria and Bait Shop.*

"Here you are, kids!" said Mr. Watson. "Enjoy yourselves!"

Peter got out and held the car door for Rosemary. She raised her eyebrows, but did not comment.

Mr. Watson leaned out the car window. "And don't do anything I wouldn't do!" he said, giving Peter a nod and a wink.

He drove off, leaving Peter staring. "I wish he wouldn't do that."

"He's my father," said Rosemary. "Try and stop him."

Luigi's Pizzeria and Bait Shop had last been decorated in the 1970s. Its look had only recently moved, of its own accord, from dated to retro. Battered wooden booths lined one wall opposite a long counter. The counter and the sides of all the tables were rimmed with black plastic and the seats and counter stools were covered in worn brown vinyl. Top 40 rock music played over the conversations. Nobody cared that it was too bright. Everything was spotless, and was kept that way by the proprietor, who greeted Peter at the door.

"Peter!" exclaimed the portly, silver-haired man.

"Hi, Luigi," said Peter. "Two, please."

"I can see that," said Luigi. "And who is this with you, this goddess, this vision? Why, can it be little Rosie Watson? You grow taller every day! I remember when you barely went up to my knee, but you still have the cutest cheeks!"

Rosemary gave Luigi a long-suffering scowl as he pinched her cheek. "I have a little sister, you know. Why don't you do this to her?"

"Well, your little sister isn't here, is she?" Luigi beamed at them. "Come on, come on! I'll show you to your booth!"

Some patrons' heads had turned during this exchange. Most were students at Clarksbury High. Some snickered as Peter and Rosemary passed. Others nodded in greeting or said hello. Peter acknowledged everyone with a smile and a nod.

They were seated at a booth three-quarters of the way to the back. Peter ordered a deluxe pizza.

"Great!" said Luigi. "With anchovies?"

"No, Luigi," said Peter.

"Are you sure? We have plenty of anchovies."

"Hold the anchovies."

Luigi smiled, patted Peter on the head, and departed, leaving the two alone to talk.

"He's gone to sneak in some anchovies, hasn't he?" said Peter.

Rosemary peered over his shoulder. "No, he's staying away from the bait fridge this time." She looked at him. "So, what's the occasion?"

Peter blinked. "What do you mean?"

"It's Tuesday. Pizza on Tuesday makes me wonder what's up."

"Nothing's up. Can't I take my friend out to pizza whenever I want?"

"I suppose." They paused as Luigi cut in, delivering drinks. Rosemary sipped her soda. Peter noticed that she was not wearing her usual bulky grey cardigan, but a tighter, fuzzy green sweater that complemented her eyes, among other things.

She sighed, breaking him from his reverie. "It's not like I have any other dates."

Peter frowned at her. "What do you mean?"

"Well, look at me. Nobody's lined up to date me."

Peter snorted. Rosemary looked hurt. "It's not *that* funny."

"No, it's just wrong," said Peter. "You'd be a great date."

Now Rosemary snorted. "Come on. I'm a geek. I'm a short geek. I'm a short fat geek with glasses —"

"You're not fat!"

"What? You're not going to argue with the rest of it?"

She rubbed her right palm idly. Peter saw the blue spot like a birthmark at the centre of it, the only sign of the adventure they'd shared three years before when she'd dipped her hand in the Sea of Ink and faced down dozens of hostile characters.

I've faced death with her, he thought. I can face telling her the truth. Can't I?

"Look ...." He took a deep breath, then the plunge. "You're pretty, okay? You're just the right size, and you have nice cheeks. I like your glasses and the way that one corner of your mouth is higher than the other. You've got nice ...." He suddenly realized he was cupping his hands out in front of him, and that Rosemary was staring at them in horror. "Um ... ears! And I like the way you blush, and how you're so serious when you're reading and you don't think I'm watching you, and ... and ..."

He stopped when he saw Rosemary giving him a look that was equal parts pleasure, shock, embarrassment, and panic. And tipping towards panic. The noise level in the restaurant had dropped several decibels.

He sat on his hands. "And I think you're pretty. Yeah. That's what I think."

Rosemary flushed and looked away. "Thanks," she said quietly. She curled up into herself for a moment, and then gave Peter a quick look. "Really?"

"Really."

Silence followed. They fidgeted. Finally, Peter coughed and said, "Nice place here."

"Yes!" Rosemary clutched at the line like a drowning swimmer. "It's been here as long as I can remember. Luigi always likes to embarrass me, but he's got a good place. Everybody goes here. I bet you wouldn't see anything like it in Toronto."

"I wouldn't know," said Peter. "My parents weren't big on eating out. If there was no time to cook, they went for a cheap fast-food chain. Plenty of those in Toronto."

Rosemary looked at him seriously. "What was it like? You've never told me about it. How do you sleep with all that noise?"

Peter rolled his straw in his fingers. "You get used to it," he said at last. "I had trouble sleeping when I first came here. Clarksbury was *too* quiet."

"How can anything be too quiet?"

"You get used to the noises. You take them into yourself and make them a part of your sleep. The rumble of streetcars outside your window, the footsteps, conversations, all of it. Those are the sounds your mind needs to say that everything is all right. You miss it when it goes."

Rosemary stared at him across the table. There was something about her expression that made Peter flush and look away.

"Was it hard coming here?" she asked, carefully. "Leaving all that behind?"

He sucked his lips. "Er ... yes ... and no. It helped that my uncle was here. I hadn't spent more than two weeks with any one foster family before that. My uncle may not be around much, but at least I have a house to go home to."

Rosemary started to say something, but Luigi arrived, delivering a steaming pizza and telling both to "watch out, it's hot." Peter changed the subject the moment Luigi stepped away; but he kept casting glances at Rosemary as she ate.

***

"Let's not call my dad," said Rosemary as she stepped out onto the street. "It's a wonderful night."

Peter didn't hear her. He stared across the street. A shadow was standing in the lamplight, slender and feminine and odd.

She's standing in the light, thought Peter. Why is she in shadow?

A car hissed past. Peter blinked, and found himself staring at a young tree, its branches shifting in the breeze.

Before he had a chance to think on this further, Rosemary took his arm and pulled him towards home. They walked in silence. Rosemary took deep breaths of the autumn air and scuffed through piles of leaves on the sidewalk.

Peter kept glancing back. He saw only trees, nothing on the street that shouldn't have been there. When they reached the end of town and turned onto the road that branched off the highway and ascended the escarpment to their homes, he took a long look back along the main road through Clarksbury. A lonely van honked at them as it passed.

The sense of being followed continued as they puffed up the slope.

Peter cast one more look behind him, and stopped dead.

Rosemary stopped when she realized she was walking ahead alone. She came back.

"I didn't realize," said Peter. "I've never walked this road this late. It's beautiful."

They stared down the 45th Parallel Road. Clarksbury clung to a thin space between the escarpment and Georgian Bay. This late at night, Georgian Bay was normally an expanse of black, broken only by isolated lights of boats straggling home, and occasionally a Great Lakes freighter. Now the bay was white. A low cloud swept over Clarksbury, taking on the orange glow of the streetlights.

"Fog's rolling in," said Rosemary.

Peter nodded. "Toronto's got nothing on this."

Rosemary took his hand. Peter felt his fingers tingle in her grip. He looked at her face, and he forgot all about looking behind him.

"Come on," she said. "Dad will be getting worried."

Holding hands, they walked the rest of the way home, reaching the top of the escarpment and enjoying the fresh breeze and the clear night sky. He saw her to her mailbox, then hesitated as he said goodbye.

"Are you all right, Peter?"

"Listen ...." He struggled for the right words. "I just wanted to thank you. You're a really good friend. High school and Clarksbury would be a lot lonelier without you."

She smiled. "Come on, Peter. I should be thanking you. People don't tease me nearly so much as they would if I weren't ... you know ... around you."

"Whatever the case, thank you," he said. And impulsively, he hugged her.

She hugged him back. "You're welcome."

Then Peter tilted Rosemary's chin up, lowered his head, and kissed her, gently, on the lips.

The scent of her washed over him. He thought it was a wonderful perfume, but then he realized that Rosemary didn't wear perfume. The feel of her lips against his felt like the most right thing in the world.

Rosemary's arms went around him. She pressed up against him and her hands traced his shoulder blades. He held the kiss and breathed her in. He could hear his pulse rush like the ocean ...

Suddenly Rosemary tensed beneath him. She planted her hands on his chest and pushed away. She stared at him in shock.

Peter felt the colour drain from his cheeks.

I've ruined it, he thought. I've ruined it all.

He let go. "Oh! God! I'm sorry!"

"It's okay," said Rosemary. "It's okay."

"I got ... I didn't ... I'd better go home, now."

"I'll see you tomorrow?" There was a nervous edge to Rosemary's question.

"Yeah," said Peter, backing away. "See you tomorrow." He turned away and walked so fast down the country road, he was almost running.

***

Rosemary stood on her porch, staring down the road where Peter had gone. She touched her lips, wondering why they tingled so. "What just happened?"

Peter just kissed me, her mind replied. He. Kissed. Me. And I freaked. Why? For seven-eighths of the time it felt so right. And then it felt so ...

After another moment of staring, Rosemary

slipped inside. She brushed past her father's greeting and went directly to her room, where she stood in front of her computer, her hand hesitating on the keyboard. In the window behind, she could see fog rising up the escarpment. Clarksbury was just an orange glow.

She took her hand off the keyboard. "No. This is too personal for e-mail." She sat at her drafting table desk and dug out a pad of graph paper. She chewed the cap clean off her pen before she finally began to write.

Peter,
This isn't an easy letter for me to write. You're one of (she crossed this out and replaced it with) *You are the most special friend I've got. We've been through so much and you mean so much to me. I don't want to risk that.*

Which is why I freaked out. I guess I'm scared. I don't want you to change from my friend to my boyfriend, only to have us break up and lose everything.

She paused for a long time, tapping the nib of her pen on the paper. Then she added:

I think we should stay like we are. Our friendship is something I cherish more than anything else, and I

don't want to mess it up. I hope you understand.
Your friend,
Rosemary

Rosemary read over the letter and then folded it and slid it into an envelope. She sealed it and wrote "Peter" on the front. Then she sat for a long time, staring out her window and tapping the envelope against her lips.

The lips that Peter had kissed.

She closed her eyes. "Rosemary Ella Watson, you are a complete and utter *idiot*!"

She tossed the letter in her wastebasket, and left the room.

The envelope sat on top of crumpled paper. Then it fluttered. As though picked up by a breeze, it lifted, and twisted through the room to Rosemary's open window. It slipped through the crack beneath the screen. Then it vanished into the night.

CHAPTER THREE
THE KNELL

There was a sickening thump.

Peter scrambled forward on the icy path, clutching his broken arm, struggling for the gate and the crowd of people surrounding the scene. He cried out for his mom and his dad, prompting some of the crowd to look at him. Arms were around him, holding him back.

"There's nothing you can do, Son!"

"Stay back! The ambulance is on its way!"

"No!" he squealed. "Mom!"

In the distance, sirens wailed.

Fog curled around his waist and blurred the faces of the people around him.

"Come home, Peter."

He turned. Fiona was standing by the gate of the park. Trees and buildings blurred in a sweeping mist until they looked like cliff faces. A lighthouse waved a wand across the sky. A foghorn wailed. A ship bell tolled.

"Come home."

Peter woke with a gasp. His clock radio was already playing. He gaped at the display.

He had missed the school bus.

***

Caught in the sunlight, Rosemary stood atop the Niagara Escarpment. Clarksbury, beneath, was covered in fog. She felt as though she was atop a mountain, looking down on clouds.

She waited at the curb, fidgeting as she watched the rolling sea of white. Finally the school bus came. She squared her shoulders and got on. She headed straight for their usual seat, and stopped.

It was empty.

Well, that was a waste of a lot of courage. How was she going to talk to Peter now?

Then the bus lurched forward and she had to sit down or risk falling over.

She slid over onto Peter's side of the seat and stared out the window until she couldn't see the other side of the road. The bus crept into town as though floating into nothingness.

Peter was not in the habit of coming to school late, but he did know he could come to school, go directly to the office, and be greeted with, at worst, raised eyebrows and the admonition not to do this again if he could help it. Whether he went to the office at ten or ten-thirty made little difference.

There was still no milk in the refrigerator. Peter settled on toast (chewed properly this time) and a tall glass of orange juice, drunk without hurry beside the kitchen table.

The radio reported fog in low-lying areas. Peter looked out his window and saw a clear blue sky.

Gathering his stuff together, he stepped out the front door, walking purposefully but without haste down his walk. He cast a quick glance at his mailbox, and stopped when he saw something inside it.

The envelope just said "Peter." He recognized Rosemary's handwriting. He ripped it open and started to read.

Moments later, he closed his eyes.

"Well. At least now I know."

* * *

Rosemary hugged her windbreaker against the chill as she walked across the school's back field. She could hardly see the building in front of her. She could hear the sounds of the harbour. A foghorn wailed. The nearest was off of Cape Croker, ten miles away. She could hear a ship bell tolling — from the Clarksbury marina, she guessed.

The ship bell tolled again. Then Rosemary heard a sound that made her stop and turn. There was a smash of wood against stone, a snap of ropes, and a plosh of objects falling into water. She heard the distant screams of men.

The other students stopped in their tracks.

"That wasn't a car crash!"

"That came from the harbour!"

"A shipwreck?"

The next sound made Rosemary imagine a tree falling. The ripping of wood and the tearing of cloth faded gradually to silence. Cape Croker's foghorn wailed again.

"What do you think we should do?" said someone. "Go for help?"

"What can we do? We're a mile from the marina."

A teacher stared in the direction of the harbour. "Students!" he said at last. "Come inside and go to your classes. When we find out what happened, we'll tell you. Come on, everybody inside."

***

The fog seemed to follow Rosemary into the school, greying her mood. She gave her history presentation, droning on Laura Secord and her heroic trek through the swamps, but her eyes were on Peter's empty desk. She thought she'd covered her unease well — everyone else was muttering about the shipwreck — but at the end of the period, Mr. Hunter pulled her aside.

"Nice presentation, Miss Watson," he said. "Could have used a bit more 'umph.'"

"Oh," she said. "Sorry."

"Something on your mind?"

She shrugged.

"About Peter?"

She felt herself blush. The feeling made her blush even more.

His frown deepened. "Want to talk about it?"

"Um ... thanks," she said. Silence stretched. She swallowed. Then the bell saved her. "Gotta go!" She pulled herself from Hunter's look and walked out into the hall faster than she'd walked all day.

It was bright in the hallway. For a minute, she blinked, and wondered if lights had flickered on, but the cloud on her mind returned and everything dimmed again.

Rosemary slogged through French, then fled into the girls' washroom. She splashed her face and cleaned her glasses. It didn't help. Her reflection looked unfocussed, her brown hair frizzy, her skin tinged grey. She rubbed her eyes and wondered why she was so tired. Last night she'd been restless, but she'd slept. This morning she'd been so keyed up about talking to Peter about their — she swallowed — relationship, that she could hardly sit still. It wasn't until she'd come in from the fog that the fog surrounded her.

Where *was* he? How *dare* he not be here when she so needed to talk to him?

Rosemary felt the hairs prickle at the back of her neck, and she whirled around. Nobody stood behind her. Still, the feeling of being watched didn't go away. She strained her ears to listen over the hum of the fluorescent lights, and she scanned the floor beneath the stall doors. "Is somebody there?" Silence.

She picked up her knapsack and made to go, but something brushed against the back of her neck and she whirled around again.

She found herself staring at the mirror. She was sure something had been there, behind her, reaching for her throat. But looking hard, all she saw was her reflection.

The washroom door burst open. "I'm going to kill Peter McAllister!" Brittney snapped, stomping past

Rosemary as if she wasn't there. "I'm going to murder him! They're going to find his body in the bay!"

Veronica strode in behind. The two girls began touching up their makeup in front of the mirror. "I thought Mr. Simmons would pop a vein when Peter didn't show."

"What about me?" Brittney yelled, looking up from her lipstick. "I had to give the presentation on my own!"

Rosemary's brow furrowed. Peter wouldn't miss a deadline like this. Not without calling in sick.

Her heart lurched. Maybe he *was* sick.

"Hey, Rosemary," Veronica called. "You didn't do anything to distract Peter, did y—" She turned from the mirror, but Rosemary was already gone, the door swinging shut behind her.

In the office, the administrative assistant looked up from her computer manual. "Rosemary? Is something wrong?"

Rosemary shifted on her feet in front of Miss Stevens' desk, feeling foolish and paranoid. She took a deep breath. "Could I use the phone? I've got to make a call."

"You sick or something? You need to call your folks?"

"No, not sick," said Rosemary. She touched her stomach. "I've just got to call ... home. Yeah. To arrange ... things. Okay?"

Miss Stevens shrugged and nodded at the phone on the wall. "Hit nine to get an outside line." Then she returned to her manual and tapped tentatively at her keyboard.

The phone was on the wall beside the door to Principal Jenkins' office, and she had to reach to pull the receiver off the hook. She started to key in Peter's number, then stopped. She heard Peter's name through the principal's door.

"I'm worried about Peter McAllister." It was Mr. Hunter's voice.

"What's wrong?" asked Mr. Jenkins.

"His marks are dropping," Hunter replied. "He's showing less interest in class. He's isolating himself from others."

"Teenagers. There's no cure," said Jenkins.

"Something's different," said Hunter. "If he'd been like this after coming to Clarksbury, I'd expect it, but not now. It's been too long. Rosemary Watson is worried about him, too."

"I'm sure you're overreacting," said Jenkins. "Have you talked to him?"

"He ditched school today," said Mr. Hunter. "I tried calling him, but nobody's answering the phone."

Rosemary put the phone on the hook and slipped out.

***

The ride back on the bus was quiet. The fog and the sound of the shipwreck put a pall on everyone's mood. Most just sat and stared out the windows. Rosemary sat in Peter's seat again, and sighed.

One student had a radio and was listening to the news about the shipwreck. Everyone could hear the report that emergency crews were trawling the coves between Clarksbury and Cape Croker, looking for the downed ship but turning up nothing. Not even wreckage.

"The fog is getting in the way of our investigation," said a firefighter the station had found for comment. "But we have all of our boats out on a search. If a ship went down today, we'll find it."

If, thought Rosemary. He's not sure a ship went down. He's as confused as we are.

The fog lifted as Rosemary left the bus, but she brooded through the rest of the afternoon. She ate dinner in silence. She dried the dishes listlessly. She sat in the living room but she couldn't keep her attention on the book. Finally, she set the book aside and muttered, "It has to be done."

"What was that, Rosie?" asked her father.

"I'm going for a walk," she announced, pulling on her shoes before her father had a chance to comment.

She pulled up her collar against the nippy air. On top of the escarpment, the sky remained clear, with the first stars coming out in the autumn twilight.

She walked briskly, because she knew that if she slowed down, her nerves might make her turn around and go back. As she walked, she muttered to herself.

"Peter, we have to talk."

Firm and to the point. Possibly too grim.

"Peter, can we talk?" she tried again.

Too wishy-washy.

"Peter, can I have a word with you?"

I'd never say that.

She sighed. Perhaps the words will come when I see Peter at the door.

Biting back her fears, she quickened her pace.

She found Peter on his driveway, bouncing a basketball and practising a lay-up. The ball went clean through the hoop above the garage. He caught the ball on its first bounce and went straight back into that same lay-up. His face was sullen, his movements mechanical.

"Peter?"

Another run. Another lay-up. Another basket.

"Peter!"

Another run. Another basket.

Rosemary caught his arm as he passed. "Peter, are you okay?"

He stopped and held the basketball under one arm. He gave her a cold look. "I'm fine."

She stared at him in surprise. "Why didn't you come to school today? People were worried about you."

"I wasn't up for school today," he said.

"Are you sick?"

"No."

"Something's wrong, isn't it? Please tell me, I'm your friend."

"Oh, absolutely. A friend." He began bouncing the basketball. "A good friend." Bounce. "A special friend." Bounce. "Just a friend."

"What are you talking about?" She grabbed the ball from his hands. "Why are you so upset? Was it something I said?"

"No. You said nothing. You made yourself quite clear. I appreciated the honesty, though I wish you had told me to my face."

"What do you mean?"

But Peter ignored her question. "I'm sorry I freaked you out. Maybe I wasn't ready, but I thought you were. You seemed to like being kissed for the first few minutes at least. I'm sorry I was wrong."

Peter's words sounded so familiar. With a jolt she realized why.

"How did you —" she stammered. "Peter, you weren't supposed to see that letter!"

"Wasn't I? What was I supposed to do, then? Stand around in the dark while you worked out your feelings?"

"Peter, I —"

"Well, what am I? A friend? Boyfriend?

49

Acquaintance?" He snatched back his ball. "When you've decided what you want us to be, tell me. You know what my address is. I'd give you my fax number, except I don't have one!"

Rosemary flared. "Fine! And when you're ready for a mature conversation, give me a call! I'll be waiting!" She stormed off down the road.

Peter's glare faltered and he made to follow her, but he checked himself. After a moment's hesitation, he threw one more basket, and then kicked the basketball into a corner of the yard. He stormed inside.

＊＊

"Who mailed my letter to Peter?" Rosemary shouted as she burst through her front door. "Was it you, Trisha? Was it?"

Her little sister dropped her fork with a clatter.

Her father stood up. "Rosemary, calm down. What's wrong?"

"Wrong? Somebody in this house delivered a letter Peter wasn't supposed to see! It said all the wrong things!"

"Rosie, what are you talking about?" said her father. "What letter? What's wrong with Peter?"

"Peter's furious! My letter told him I just wanted to be friends with him."

"But you're already ...." Mr. Watson pushed up his glasses. "Oh!"

Rosemary beat her hands against her sides. "What he must think of me! And after I was ready to tell him how I felt. It's all ruined!"

"Rosemary, I'm sure it will be all right if you just give things time —"

"Time?! Peter and I have had three years! Why didn't I see this happening? Why wasn't I ready? Why was I so stupid? Why didn't anybody tell me?"

"Rosemary, I —"

Rosemary's eyes were glistening now. Her voice quivered. "And now Peter thinks that I don't love him, and I do, and he doesn't love me, and I'm so confused, and everything is ruined, and you don't understand, and I can't take it anymore!" She could hold back the tears no longer. She ran to her room, slamming the door behind her. She flung herself onto her bed and cried into her pillow.

After a while, there was a soft knock at her door.

"Go away!" she yelled.

The door opened with a click and Rosemary's mother sidled in. She sat at the edge of her bed and brushed back her daughter's hair until Rosemary was through crying.

"I'm sorry I shouted at Dad," said Rosemary at last. "Is he angry?"

"No. Befuddled, but not angry. He muttered something about not understanding women. I'll have a few words with him about that."

"And Trish?"

"Not affected at all. She's playing with her helicopter."

Rosemary chuckled. "Good ol' unflappable Trish." Then she curled up into herself. "I'm so embarrassed! It was like I wasn't even there. I couldn't stop myself from blurting out that I was in love with Peter ... to my father, no less!"

"Rosemary, dear, that isn't news to us."

Rosemary rolled over and looked at her mother. "It's not?"

Her mother laughed. "It's plain as day. The whole town knows. Except you two, apparently."

Rosemary flushed. "I thought they were just teasing us!" She frowned. "Oh, dear."

Her mother smiled. "It's about time you saw what was in front of you. That's why I can tell you that it's going to be okay."

"But Mom, I wrote him a letter that told him that I wanted us to just stay friends!"

"Then you'll just have to tell him otherwise. I'm sure he won't mind if you change your mind. Peter may not know it, but he loves you as much as you love him. If you're courageous enough, you'll get over this rough spot. I think that you two deserve each other."

She sat up. "You *wanted* me to date Peter? My best friend?! Moms aren't supposed to do that! Dad's teasing was bad enough!"

"Well, your dad might have to change his approach," said her mother. "Depending on what you two do, there could be a man-to-man talk with Peter in the near future."

Rosemary winced. "Poor Peter."

Her mother chuckled. "Your dad does love to play the clichés." She squeezed Rosemary's shoulder. "Consider yourself lucky I waited this long. You could have had me matchmaking."

***

Rosemary spent the rest of the evening reading *War for the Oaks* by Emma Bull. Finally, at ten, she finished her chapter and cringed. "Poor Eddi." She marked her place and set the book on her bedside table.

She undressed and slipped into a long t-shirt. She washed and brushed her teeth and, returning, hesitated a moment at her door. Across the hall from her, Theo's room stood open. Bed made, floor clean, everything so tidy it screamed emptiness.

Maybe I can catch him on instant messenger, she thought. Ask him what to do.

She wrinkled her nose. Ask my older brother for

boy advice? We'd hear his screams all the way from Toronto. But I guess it's less weird than getting boy advice from Mom. Slightly less weird.

She shut the door and stared a moment out her window. The view to the bay was still a sea of grey.

I can figure this out on my own. I'll talk to Peter tomorrow, she thought. If he doesn't show up at school, I'll talk to him at home. I'll apologize, and then I'll invite him over for dinner.

And if the first conversation goes well, we'll have more to talk about. And we'll need some place to do that alone. Back at his place? Or possibly the woods. Hmm ... kissed beside a sink of dirty dishes, or under an autumn canopy? Definitely the woods.

She cast one more glance out her window.

She blinked. A waft of cloud rose from the top of the fog and moved towards her, pushed by a sudden wind, like a white schooner making sail.

She shook her mind clear. Her imagination was playing tricks again.

Rosemary drew the blinds and climbed into bed.

***

Peter jabbed the remote control to turn the television off. The house fell silent. He could hear his breathing again and he knew it was going to keep him awake. But in the end, he decided that bed was the only option. His joints ached from lack of sleep.

After washing and brushing, he slipped into sweat-pants and slid under the covers. He spent the next several minutes staring at the ceiling.

"I'm such an idiot," he said at last.

Rosemary is never going to speak to you again.

I've got to call her. Tell her I'm sorry.

It's one-thirty in the morning. Call her tonight, and she'll really never speak to you again.

Tomorrow. I'll talk to her tomorrow. If she'll let me. Maybe if I corner her at her parents', she'll let me.

Peter fluffed his pillow. But sleep still would not come.

Something shone in his eyes: a bright light through the window.

Darn moon, he thought. Must be full. I thought that wasn't for a whole week. Why now? I'm almost asleep. Let me sleep, moon, please?

"I should have pulled the blinds," he muttered.

The light faded. Darkness covered his eyes.

"That's better," he whispered as sleep took him.

Silhouetted in the moonlight, a feminine form clung to the window frame.

***

There was a sickening thump.

Peter ran for the park gates, screaming for his mom and dad. He slipped on the icy pathway.

Then Rosemary appeared from nowhere and grabbed him before he hit the ground.

The boy of nine stared in awe at the girl of fifteen. She took one look at him and drew him into a close embrace, shushing him gently. Her shoulder was soon wet with his tears.

The shattered light from the ice-covered willow shimmered over them. The frozen branches shifted with wooden clacks. A blurry shape stepped close. Blinking away the wash of tears, Peter saw Fiona standing over Rosemary's shoulder, her hands on her hips.

Then she vanished into smoke. A dense fog rolled around them, and ice turned into water. Waves lapped against their boat.

Boat?

Yes, they were in a boat, so far out into Georgian Bay that the escarpment was a black smudge on the horizon. Cape Croker's lighthouse shot a pinprick of light towards them at regular intervals.

Neither had lifejackets. Rosemary sat back and picked up the oar. She cursed under her breath as she tried to pull the boat to shore.

Cape Croker's foghorn wailed. The shore was vanishing on them, and the boat was taking on water. It soaked Rosemary's shoes, but not Peter's. His feet held on the surface of the water. He put a hand to the lake, and the surface held his palm as if it were warm ice.

Six inches were in the boat, now. Rosemary gasped in frustration and fear.

Peter stood up. He *could* stand up. The boat wasn't supporting his weight, the water was.

Rosemary squeaked as the water slipped around her waist.

Peter reached out to her.

"No!" she gasped. "Don't rock the boat! Don't —"

The boat sank like a stone. Rosemary floundered in the water. Her oar slipped out of reach.

Peter staggered on the undulating surface. He grabbed Rosemary's wrist, but her head slipped under water. He tried to pull her up, using both hands, but she was a lead weight.

Bubbles seeped from her lips and frothed on the surface. Her hair fluttered like seaweed. Her hand grew cold and slipped from his fingers. She vanished into the depths.

And Peter was left standing, alone, in the middle of the ice-covered wading pool.

Off in the distance, sirens called to him.

* * *

Peter tangled his feet in the covers and fell hard on his bedroom floor. Cursing, he struggled free and staggered out of his room, down the stairs (missing the last two and barely saving himself on the railing) and into the kitchen where he almost pulled the phone out of the wall. His fingers fumbled over the numbers. It took two tries before he keyed in the right ones.

He twitched as he listened to the connection ringing, three times. Six. Nine. Twelve.

Finally, a male voice, gruff with sleep, answered. "Watson residence."

"Mr. Watson? Where's Rosemary?"

There was a pause. "Peter?" said the voice at last. "Do you have any idea what time it is?"

"Please, Mr. Watson. I have to speak to Rosemary! Have to!"

"She's asleep, you know. Peter, what's gotten into you?"

Peter drew a shaky breath. "Please?"

Something in Peter's voice must have convinced Rosemary's father, for he said, "Okay, I'll wake her. But if she comes to breakfast tomorrow grumpy, I'm going to have words with you." He set down the receiver. Peter could hear him climbing the stairs. There was a tense wait, and then Rosemary's wispy, sleep-riddled, "Hello?"

"Rosemary!" Peter exclaimed.

"Peter? What is it?"

Peter was now fully awake, and his conscious mind leapt ahead to what Rosemary would say if he told her the reason why he had called. Embarrassment overtook him. But he had to know.

"Peter?" Rosemary repeated, concerned. "Peter, what's wrong?"

"Are you okay?" he croaked at last.

"Other than being up at ...," there was a brief pause, "... three-thirty in the morning! Why are you calling me?"

Again, Peter couldn't think of a thing to say.

"Peter, I'm all right! For God's sake, what's wrong? What happened?"

"I'm sorry. I'm just — I just had a bad dream. I'm sorry I woke you."

"Peter, wait —"

Hanging up, he leaned against the kitchen wall and slid to the floor. He held his head in his hands and began to cry.

"Peter."

He hardly heard the voice. Then a hand touched his shoulder. "Peter, don't cry."

He looked up, then let out a startled yell and scrambled back along the floor.

A girl in her late teens sat against the wall, her knees drawn to her chest. She had freckled skin, green eyes, and red hair that cascaded as far down as the small of her back. Her beauty registered in Peter's mind despite his fear.

"Who ... who ...," he stammered. "How did you ...." Then he realized there was something familiar about this woman, and he gave her a closer look. His eyes widened.

"Fiona?!"

CHAPTER FOUR
THIS MUSIC CREPT BY ME

Rosemary stood staring at the receiver long after Peter hung up, while her sleep-addled brain struggled to think of what to do next. She tried to call Peter back, but got only busy signals. Finally, she gave up, and stood in the centre of her living room.

Should I go over to his place?

No. The idea of heading over to his house at four in the morning seemed ludicrous.

She wobbled on her feet.

Bed. I can't think out here. I have to think in bed.

Sleep overtook her as she slipped under the covers.

Tomorrow. There will be time to speak to him tomorrow.

At the edge of her consciousness, another voice agreed.

Time enough.

***

Fiona was just as Peter remembered her. She hadn't aged a day since she'd babysat a nine-year-old boy who'd had a serious crush on her.

She was smiling at him. He remembered that smile.

"Fiona," Peter breathed. "I haven't seen you for ...." Not since the accident, he realized. "How did you get in here?"

"You let me in," said Fiona. "When you called to me in your dream."

Peter gaped at her.

"Don't be afraid," she said. "I've come to bring you home."

He was still staring at her. He could feel himself doing it, but he couldn't help it. She shone like the moon in fog.

She produced a steaming mug and held it out to him. "Coffee?"

It was the furthest thing from his mind. "What?"

"To help you think," she said.

He took the coffee and gulped it. He gaped at the mug. "Hey, we're out of coffee! How —"

She drew herself up gracefully. "Peter. Do you really want to ask about the coffee first?"

"Uh ...," he said. "No, I ...." Then he shook his

head until it rattled. "How did you get in here? Who are you? What are you talking about, 'home'?"

"Home, Peter. To your family."

"What family? I haven't got a family, except for ...." He didn't say his uncle's name. "What are you *talking* about?"

"Your *real* family, Peter. Our family. We have lived in the water, the shoreline our playground, since before people settled here. You are one of us. You are not human."

"Excuse me?!"

"Come on, Peter. You know you don't belong here. I've watched you. You play their games; you pass their tests; you live among them — but you are not one of them. Can't you feel it?"

Peter took a breath to contradict her, then stopped.

She's nuts, he told himself. But ... but she knew about my dream. She's been in my dreams, and now here she is in front of me. Maybe *I'm* nuts. Would I even know?

"Keep talking," he found himself saying.

"We put you with your parents," she replied. "Your parents' real baby was stillborn. We switched you with their child."

"Why?"

"To spare them their loss," she replied, "and to give you the benefits of a human upbringing."

Peter's eyes glazed over as he pictured it: his parents, not really his parents, smiling and cooing over his infant self. Living with them, being human, growing older.

A horn blared. A pickup truck slid forward, its wheels locked. There was a sickening thump.

Peter shuddered.

"I've been looking for you since we realized you were alone," said Fiona. "I've looked for years." There was something wrong about what Fiona said, but Peter couldn't process it. As much as he tried, his mind grew foggy.

"And now," said Fiona, "I can bring you home."

"Home," he said, and shook his head.

"The water is your home. You belong with us."

He almost laughed but was afraid he wouldn't be able to stop. "What, I can't just visit for Christmas and Easter?"

"I don't understand."

"Look," said Peter. "This is crazy. I'm not going anywhere with you. I can't go live in the lake. I belong here."

Her lips tightened. "Are you sure?"

"Of course I'm sure."

Her emerald eyes bored into him. His uncle's phone message echoed in his mind, and he thought of the silence of many nights alone. Then he remembered the bitter singe of Rosemary's letter, and his words started to sound hollow to his ears.

"I can't go. How am I going to explain where I'm going?"

"Don't explain. Just go."

"But my friends will miss me," said Peter. "Like Benson and Joe and ... and ... and then there's Rosemary."

She smiled at him sadly. "Ah, yes, Rosemary. Is she all that you want her to be?"

Peter bit his lip. After a moment, he said, "She'd miss me if I left."

She smiled, but there was a shadow behind her eyes. "Then you had better get ready for school, and see your friends."

"What —"

A flash made Peter turn around. He had to shield his eyes against the light streaming through the front windows. It couldn't be morning already, could it?

He turned back, but Fiona was gone. He sat alone, a cold cup of coffee by his hand.

His clock radio turned on in his room.

The house echoed with emptiness.

***

Rosemary stood yawning at her mailbox. The sun shone, but the air was still and damp. Further down the hill, the fog shrouded Clarksbury from sight.

The mailbox door squeaked as she flipped it open and closed.

Inside the plastic newspaper delivery box below the mailbox was a copy of the *Owen Sound Sun-Times*. The headline reported that the search for the mysterious shipwreck had been called off until the fog lifted. Rosemary looked at the fog and sighed.

The yellow school bus drew up at the opposite curb. Slamming the mailbox door closed, she crossed the road. She hesitated at the open doors, took a deep breath, and climbed in.

In the midst of chattering students, Rosemary focussed on Peter in his seat. He was staring out the window, bags under his eyes.

Stepping up the aisle, she stumbled as the bus lurched forward. She was barely able to grab a hand-hold and swing herself into her seat, jostling Peter. "Sorry," she gasped. Peter said nothing.

Rosemary stared ahead, twisting her hands while the bus slipped into the fog. Despite the shouted conversations around her, silence hovered over Peter like a cloud. When she had the strength to break it, all she could say was, "So ..."

Peter said nothing.

Rosemary sighed. "Look. I'm sorry about ... um ...." She curled up into herself. "I just freaked, that's all."

She clenched her fists and shifted in her seat. Finally, she said, "Look, I don't even know how you got that letter. I didn't send it. I threw it in the wastebasket. I didn't even really mean to write it, but I was overwhelmed. That didn't mean I didn't like being kissed."

She waited for a response. "Peter? Are you listening to me?"

The bus juddered to a stop. The students grabbed their bags. Peter stood up and tripped over Rosemary's feet. He stared at her as though she had appeared out of nowhere.

"Peter?"

He glared at her, then followed the flow of students.

"Peter!" Rosemary started after him, but a hand clapped her shoulder and pulled her back.

"Hey!" She struggled to turn. The back of the bus was empty. One of her backpack's straps had caught itself on the seat, pinning her shoulder. She pulled free, disentangled the straps, and ran out into the schoolyard, looking for Peter.

The other students were milling around, grey shapes in the fog, looking about in bewilderment. Joe was closest to her. "What the heck —"

Then she heard it. A shush in the trees, a sound that played across the back of her mind. Whispers off the building walls. She couldn't make out the words.

Veronica shuddered. "Stupid fog."

Rosemary caught sight of Peter, walking on ahead, oblivious to the voices. The fog gathered around him as he reached the school doors, and he vanished from sight.

***

In French class, Peter glowered at his desk.

Rosemary had ignored him. Okay, perhaps she was angry at being woken up in the middle of the night, but to say nothing? To sit somewhere else? That hurt.

I've driven her away, he thought. She never felt for me the way I felt for her.

"Peter?" Madame Krug stood pointing to the assignment on the board.

Quietest trip ever on that bus. Not one person bothered to say hello.

"Peter? Are you all right?"

I might as well be invisible, the way people treat me.

"Peter!"

Peter jerked to attention.

"Peter, where are you today, off in some cloud?" the teacher asked. The classroom snickered.

"Sorry," said Peter.

"*Je m'excuse, madame, s'il vous plait*, Peter," said Madame Krug.

Peter coughed. "*Je m'excuse*, Madame Krug." He slumped in his seat. It was going to be a long day.

***

Rosemary waited by her locker between classes. Her eyes scanned the passing students.

Around her, people whispered about the fog.

"This is getting creepy," said Brittney. "First that shipwreck, and now those voices? That's not the wind playing tricks with us."

"Sure it is," said Joe. "What else could it be?"

"Ghosts, of course," said Benson.

Veronica glowered into her locker. "Shut up, Benson!"

"No, seriously. There's, like, a ton of shipwrecks around here, right?" Benson went on. "Well, ask yourself: how come?"

"Rocks," said Brittney.

"But there's the lighthouse and maps and stuff," Benson pressed. "There's gotta be more to it."

"Like what?" Brittney rolled her eyes. "Magnets?"

"No, sirens. Drawing the sailors onto the rocks."

"Sirens?" said Joe.

"Yeah, you know, creatures like beautiful women. Sort of sexy water vampires, like the *Brides of Dracula*?" Benson's face took on a distant, contented look.

Veronica slammed her locker door.

"This is stupid! You're being stupid!" She stood with her hands on her hips. "It's just some freaky weather, that's all!"

Then Rosemary spotted Peter. "Peter!" She waved. "Peter!" When he didn't answer, she darted towards him and plucked him from the stream. "Peter!"

Behind her, Joe said to Benson, "Sirens would be cool. You think they raised the fog?"

Rosemary pulled Peter out of the others' earshot. He glared at her. "What do you want?"

"I've been trying to talk to you!"

"What about?"

"We have to talk, Peter. About the letter —"

"That letter made things perfectly clear, Rosemary."

"I wasn't going to send it. I was going to talk to you."

"Yeah, well, I appreciate the personal touch."

"What is wrong with you?" she whispered. "Do you want me to say 'I love you'? Well, I can't!" She cast a quick glance to make sure the others weren't eavesdropping. They weren't. She turned back to Peter. "Not yet. I've never felt this way before. I don't know how I should feel. But I want to find out, if you do."

She gave Peter what she hoped was an encouraging smile. That changed to a look of astonishment as Peter stared at her, wide-eyed and on the verge of tears.

He turned and walked away with the stride that tried very hard not to be a run. Rosemary backed into her locker door.

Behind her, Veronica had opened her locker again, and was sorting around for a missing textbook. The bell rang.

"C'mon, B," said Joe. "We'll be late for practice."

"Yeah," said Benson. "See you, Rosemary!" He gave her a wave. Then he tiptoed behind Veronica and whispered in her ear. "See you, Veronica!"

Veronica jerked up with a shriek. The back of her head caught Benson square on the nose.

"Benson!" she yelled. "Don't do that to me again!"

"Sorry," he mumbled, clutching his nose.

Veronica gathered up her books and stormed off to class.

★★★

The afternoon just got worse. Everybody was whispering behind his back.

"*His marks are dropping,*" Hunter replied. "*He's showing less and less interest in class. He's isolating himself from others.*"

They all think I'm a failure.

"*Do you want me to say 'I love you'? Well, I can't!*"

Then, several decibels lower:

"I've never felt this way before. I don't know how I should feel. But I want to find out."

Peter shook his head, trying to clear it. Rosemary didn't say that. I wouldn't be nearly this angry if she had.

"Peter? Look alive, there! You're up!"

Peter dribbled his basketball. He ran for his lay-up, jumped, missed.

"Good hustle, Peter," shouted Coach Beckett. "More focus, next time. Try again."

Peter faced the basket.

"I don't want you to change from my friend to my boyfriend, only to have us break up and lose everything."

The ball hit his toe and skittered to the wall. Where had *that* thought come from?

"Keep trying, Peter," shouted Joe. "You'll get it!"

Peter grabbed the ball, picked up his pace, rounding on the basket ...

Rosemary, kissing, tensing, then pushing him away ...

The basketball bounced off the rim. Peter swore loudly.

His classmates stared. Coach Beckett scowled. "Only losers swear, Peter."

Peter threw down the basketball and stormed off.

"Peter?" Joe started after him.

"Peter? What's wrong?" Coach Beckett put a hand on Peter's shoulder, but Peter shook it off and quickened his pace towards the outer doors.

"Peter!"

Fiona was right. Nobody cares about me. I want to go home.

The doors smashed open and he ran into the back field. The fog wrapped him, and he stood in the centre of a white void. Only then did he allow himself to cry.

"*Now do you understand?*" Fiona's voice came from everywhere and nowhere. He smelled it like the fog.

His gaze hardened. He wiped his face dry and cleared his nose with a sniff. He spoke to the air. "Where do I go from here?"

Fiona stepped into view and took his hands. "Follow me."

Holding hands, they walked out of the back field. Then they walked briskly across the road and strode down the sidewalk towards downtown Clarksbury. Nobody passed them. By the time they hit the main street, they were running full tilt.

***

Rosemary meandered through the book stacks. Study period — right. No way could she study. Every window she passed was a featureless square of white. She stared out at the fog, remembering the voices, the sound of the shipwreck. And Peter acting so weird.

There was so much on her mind — but the only thing she could look up was shipwrecks. She picked *A History of the Bruce Peninsula* off the shelf and scanned the index. Shipwrecks.

There were hundreds.

Shipwrecks, maps of, 107. On page 107 a familiar shoreline jumped out at her. Her home, scattered with red crosses. A green square marked Fathom Five National Marine Park. The red crosses, marking shipwrecks, ran up and down the shore. Five were clustered around Clarksbury Harbour.

She turned back to the index, scanned down the two columns of tiny type. Shipwrecks, siren legends about, 209.

> The USS *Lorelei* was sailing Lake Huron when the War of 1812 broke out. Trapped in unfriendly waters, the *Lorelei* ran. The ship's captain, Glenn Hoskins, raced narrow passages and hid in rocky shallows where the British dared not follow.
>
> Survivors report that the crew began to hear voices, whispering off the cliffs and water.

Rosemary looked out the fog-soaked window. Voices.

A fog rose up around the ship, but Hoskins, as if suicidal, raced the channels blind. His crew mutinied. Hoskins and his officers tricked them into going below decks with the promise of a meeting. Then they nailed the hatch shut. As they finished, the ship struck rock and started to sink. There was no time to pry up the nails.

Rosemary remembered the smash of wood, the snap of ropes, and the plosh of things falling into water. Distant screams.

Hoskins lashed himself to the wheel to go down with his ship, but some of the officers escaped. They surrendered to the British, who conducted a search.

They came upon a patch of water that bubbled as though there was a ship below, leaking air. As they had no way of going underwater to recover the drowned crew, they left the *Lorelei* in its final resting place. Years later, ships passing the site reported that the water still bubbled. A legend developed that sirens had driven the captain mad.

Rosemary looked at the map. The final resting place of the *Lorelei* was just outside Clarksbury Harbour.

She shook herself.

Come on. Get real, Rosemary. Peter's mad about the letter. You don't have to go all Mulder about it. There hasn't been a shipwreck on the Bruce in — the Scully in her flipped through the pages — decades.

Until, of course, yesterday. The voices. The weird noises.

She snapped the book closed.

As she put the book back on the shelf, she caught sight of the ink-blot birthmark on her palm, the only reminder of the adventure that had brought her and Peter together in the first place. She stared at it a moment, and then looked out the window at the fog. Her eyes narrowed.

The bell rang. Rosemary shouldered her knapsack and ran for the buses.

***

When Rosemary got back on the school bus, her eyes tracked to the seat she shared with Peter. She blinked to find it empty. Then she was pushed by the students filing in behind her. Stumbling to the back of the bus, she slid into Peter's place.

She stared out the fog-shrouded window, barely able to see the passing sidewalks, not listening to the conversations around her, until she heard Peter's name.

"What was Peter's problem, today?" asked Benson, who sat two seats down from her. He was talking to Joe. "Just throwing down his ball and running out of the gym? What got into him?"

"Maybe he and Rosemary had a fight." Veronica shot Rosemary a snide grin.

"Shut up, Veronica," said Benson.

Joe shrugged. "I don't know. Coach Beckett shouted all over the back field, but he couldn't find him. He's always been a bit of a loner, but that was just strange. Rosemary, do you know what's going on?"

Rosemary stared at the inquisitive looks of Benson and Joe. They were serious and concerned, completely different from the two boys who used to take special pleasure in pelting her with snowballs.

"I ... I don't know," she managed, finally. "He's been having trouble sleeping."

Joe sighed. "That sucks. Maybe I shouldn't take 'no' for an answer when I invite him to the team party."

Veronica snorted. "At the Homecoming Dance? He wouldn't go unless Rosemary dragged him!"

Benson and Joe looked at Rosemary. "That's an idea. You want to drag him?"

Rosemary started to protest, but stopped. "Okay," she said at last. "I'll talk to him."

"Great!" said Joe.

The conversation moved on. Rosemary stared out the window as the bus reached the edge of town. The people they passed were shrouded shadows, almost unrecognizable.

But she recognized Peter when she saw him.

She pressed her face to the window. Peter was on the sidewalk, holding hands with —

What on Earth?!

The bus shuddered to a stop. Benson and Veronica got up to get off. Rosemary gathered her things and darted after them, almost knocking Benson over as she leapt to the sidewalk.

"Hey!" Veronica shouted. "Watch it!"

"Rosemary, what's the matter with you?" said Benson.

Rosemary ran to get behind the bus even as it pulled away.

They were at the crossroads where the 45th Parallel Road ascended the escarpment to Peter and Rosemary's homes. Peter could barely be seen on the other side of the road, walking with a thickening of the fog. He'd been walking with a person, hadn't he? Where was he going? He should be turning right to head home, but he was turning left, towards the bay.

"What's he doing?" said Rosemary. "Peter!"

"What's going on?" asked Benson. "What about Peter?"

Rosemary ignored them. "He can't be going to the Point. Not in this fog!"

"What?" said Benson.

Rosemary ran across the road. Benson and Veronica vanished behind her.

***

"Fiona!" Peter gasped. "Slow down! I can't keep up this pace!"

They were on a dirt track that was changing to a rugged trail that climbed the escarpment. Peter stumbled on the stony, uneven ground.

Fiona giggled. She wouldn't let go of his hand. She tugged him, playful and insistent. They hadn't met a single person, on foot or in a car, but he couldn't think on the strangeness of this while Fiona kept up the pace.

"We must hurry, Peter," she breathed. "The portal awaits!"

"Portal? What portal?"

The fog veiled all. Peter could barely see where to put his feet on the ground. He could no longer tell where he was in relation to the road, but he could hear the sounds of waves against a rocky shore, and the squeal of seagulls, and he figured they must be approaching Clark's Point.

The pathway levelled out and they stepped onto a ledge. The rocks of the escarpment rose sheer on his right, topping out ten feet above him. On his left, the ground dropped away to nothing. The ledge curved away in front, making his small patch of land look like the only solid ground in existence. Somewhere beneath the sea of white the waves of Georgian Bay rolled.

He pressed himself against the rocks, stabbed by a pang of vertigo.

Fiona smiled at him. "Don't be afraid. We're almost home."

Peter stared at her. "Where?" He had a sinking sensation the answer was "down there."

"You shall see."

She let go of his hand, stepped to the edge of the cliff, threw back her head, and sang.

Fiona's voice was barely on the edge of human hearing. There was no melody. It was a chord, higher than a piccolo and more beautiful. It made the fog roll back. The water below grew more distinct until it was as though they were standing in the eye of a small hurricane.

Then Fiona leaned forward. For one heart-pounding moment, Peter thought she was falling, but she cast her arms out and jumped into the air. Her body glowed, and then flew apart into a dozen sprites of light that drifted down out of sight.

Then Fiona's voice rang in his ears. "*Now it's your turn, Peter. Come to the edge.*"

Peter leaned out and looked down. The rock wall stretched below him fifty feet. What looked sheer from the ground was full of outcroppings and protrusions of stone from this perspective. Whitecapped waves lapped at a narrow stone beach.

Vertigo tugged at him. He staggered back and gripped the wall as best he could with his hands and his back. His breath came in short, sharp gasps.

But he could hear her voice in his head. "*Come,*" it whispered. "*See, the portal is opening.*"

The compulsion to look returned. Keeping a hand on the wall, he leaned out and looked down. In the centre of the small cove, the water was bubbling and frothing, as though there was a ship beneath the waves, leaking air.

"*Come home, Peter.*"

"Peter!"

Peter whipped around. Rosemary was standing on the ledge with him, her face pale, and the knuckles of her right hand white where she gripped the rocks. She reached out with her left.

Peter fumbled with his words. "Rosemary, how ... go away. Leave me —"

Rosemary took a step towards him. "Peter, please, you don't need to do this!"

"Get out of here," Peter gasped. "I don't want you to see me."

"I'm not leaving without you!"

Peter looked down. His knees wobbled. He pitched back into the wall.

"Rosemary, get out of here!" he yelled. "I have to do this."

"No, you don't!"

"She's calling me, Rosemary! I have to go to her!"

Rosemary shouted over him. "There are people you can talk to. There are other ways you can deal with this! For God's sake, Peter, don't jump!"

Fiona's voice rang in his ears. "*Don't listen to her, Peter!*"

Peter gulped air into his lungs. He pushed away from the rock face and straightened up.

"Peter!" Rosemary was crying.

The voice grew dark. "*Enough! Come, Peter!*"

The vertigo grabbed his legs. He staggered forward, arms cartwheeling. He tilted, beyond his balance, beyond any hope of getting back. He screamed.

Rosemary leapt forward, grabbing at him. She caught his arm. Peter's stomach lurched as he saw her feet slip on the leaf-covered edge.

"No!"

Peter and Rosemary's screams echoed as they fell the fifty feet into the water.

CHAPTER FIVE
UPON THE WATERS

Rosemary floundered, struggling for air and light.

She felt herself rising through the murk, towards a shimmering ceiling. Darkness pushed in on all sides.

Rosemary rocketed out of the water. She barely had time to breathe before falling back in.

She flailed and splashed, blind with spray. Hands clasped her arms and hauled her above the waves. The wind broke against her back, breathtakingly cold.

"Peter!" she gasped.

"Find your feet," said a voice like a strict school-teacher. "Put your feet down!"

Rosemary found ground beneath her feet. She was waist deep in the cold water. A hand pressed against her back. "Now, walk," said the stern voice.

Rosemary tried. Then she bent double and threw

up water. The voice sighed and pressed her forward, marching her to the shore.

They left the water, and Rosemary collapsed onto a flat stone. She curled up into herself, retching.

"You were a fool to follow us!" It was a woman's voice, young and sweet as a girl's, but with an edge of power and age. Rosemary rolled onto her back and opened her eyes. She sat up to stare.

A woman-creature glared at her with shark's eyes. She was tall and thin, wearing green robes. Her skin was like sea glass, and her red hair was long enough to cloak her. Hair and robes billowed in the wind. She looked as though the waves would break her, but they didn't dare.

"You wake at last." The sea-woman sneered, baring white triangles of enamel. "Good."

"Who ... who are you?"

"Peter's friend."

"Where is he?"

"Safe," the sea-woman replied. "Do not concern yourself with him. Worry about yourself. You are halfway between your world and mine. I have stayed back to show you the way home."

"Wait a minute; *you* pulled Peter off that cliff?" All she had seen was Peter holding hands with a thickening of the fog, but this felt like the same being. Maybe it could take whatever shape it wanted, like something worse than a shark-woman. Rosemary swallowed hard, then squared her shoulders, and faced up to her. "You can't just take him away. That's kidnapping!"

"I am taking him home. You need to go to your home. Look around you."

The tone of her voice gave Rosemary no choice but to look around.

She was sitting on a rock at the base of a line of cliffs stretching along the shore of an endless lake. The world was bathed in perpetual twilight, with no sun or stars in the sky. The dome overhead was a smooth navy blue, broken only at the cliff tops where clouds hung as thick as the fog around Clarksbury.

"That pathway will take you home." The sea-woman pointed to a gully cut into the cliff. There was a fin growing along the back of her arm. "It is difficult terrain, but you should make it. Don't look back, for the path will vanish behind you."

Rosemary shivered in the steady wind. "I'm not leaving without Peter."

The woman's smile wasn't sympathetic. "Suit yourself. Good luck. It is a cold wind." She walked backwards into the lake. "This place echoes memories. Don't be ensnared."

"Hey!" Rosemary scrambled to her feet. "Come back here!"

The sea-woman cast up her arms and the lake rose.

The wave dodged around her and charged at Rosemary. She barely had time to clutch at her glasses before the wall of water smashed her into the cliff face. Rosemary struggled against the suck of the undertow. Stones cracked against her legs and arms. Her lungs begged for air once more. Finally, the water receded, leaving Rosemary clinging to the flat stone, gasping.

The woman was gone. The only sound was the roar of the waves, and the whistle of the wind.

When she recovered her senses, Rosemary pulled away from the shoreline. She sat on a stone and tried to dry her glasses with her sopping cardigan before she realized that was silly. Blood trickled from a cut on her knee, and her head ached. The wind was so cold it burned her skin. And somewhere a bell tolled.

"Well," she said at last. "That went well." She sat shivering as she took recent events apart and put them back together again, trying to think of what to do next.

Around her, the fog that had been at the top of the cliffs descended, wrapping around her. The rocks seemed to dissolve like candle wax.

That woman had pulled her out of a lake. Not the same lake they had fallen into, but a lake nonetheless. And the woman had stepped back into that lake before leaving. Then there was the path the woman wanted her to take, without Peter. The direct opposite to that path was the lake.

That settled it. She had to get across that lake.

But how? A boat?

The bell tolled again.

Wait a minute. Where is that bell coming from?

She looked around, holding herself against the cold, but she was surrounded by fog now. Waves rolled in from nothing and broke at her feet. But the sound of the bell was as plain as day. It echoed from the cliff face behind her, and it was getting closer.

Then black burst out from the white: a three-masted schooner in full sail, its prow already above her. Rosemary rolled away, yelling, and covered her head. The ship bucked like a wounded animal. Wood crunched against stone. Rigging fell around her, bombarding her with sound. There was a snap of ropes and the plosh of objects hitting water. The masts toppled with the sound of timber, and Rosemary heard the screams of men.

Then the screaming stopped. Rosemary chanced a look up, and then stumbled to her feet. She gaped.

There was no sign of the ship that had broken on top of her, unless the shipwreck had occurred years ago. Instead, she stood in the middle of a graveyard of snapped masts. Multiple ships rested here. Nearest her, the wooden ribcage of a stern poked above the waves. Beyond the waves, the navy blue sky could be seen through holes in the metal hull of a tanker. Planks and chunks of metal littered the shore among large cargo boxes, some made of wood and others of corrugated metal. Several of the boxes had broken open and spilled out their contents. There were no bodies.

Rosemary drew her arms around herself. Her teeth chattered. She took a step, tripped, and fell on her face.

What was wrong with her? She struggled to her hands and knees, as her legs wouldn't hold her up. Her fingers were numb. Her teeth were chattering so hard she could hardly breathe. It was so *cold*.

Cold. With a gasp, Rosemary looked at her fingertips. They had gone pale.

Hypothermia. The wind was strong and bitter. Worst of all, she was soaking wet. She needed shelter, dry clothes and a heat source. Now.

The gully looked very tempting, but to go along it meant leaving Peter behind forever. Besides, she doubted she could make it back to Clarksbury before she passed out. The means to save herself had to be here.

She stumbled among the wreckage, pulling aside planks, looking into crates. She fell several times, once into a tide pool. Each time, it was harder to get up.

Her hand fell upon something soft and she pulled it out. A blanket fluttered in the wind. She wrapped herself up, but it was too little, too late. Her fingertips were blue.

She peered into box after box, casting aside food canisters, boxes of nails, more blankets. Then, as she was about to toss aside another can, she stopped and stared at it with shaking hands.

The writing was decades old, though the metal shone like new. The words made Rosemary gasp with new hope. "S-s-st-terno!" Canned heat. She was halfway to being saved. Her eyes darted from container to container, looking for … oh, to be this close!

She let out a shuddering yell of delight and stumbled to a crate whose contents had spilled out and broken open. Thick wooden matches lay scattered about. She scooped up a dry box.

The beach had cut into the cliffs, and one could sit on stones beneath a rocky overhang, out of the wind. Rosemary ducked underneath. Using a nail, she pried open the can of Sterno and placed it on a dry stone. Her fingers could hardly hold a match, let alone strike it, but desperation drove her forward and she finally lit one. The can flared up in blue flame.

Rosemary breathed a shaky sigh of relief. She placed the flaming can just outside the overhang and started putting wood over the flames. The wood sputtered and smoked, but finally caught. The heat singed her cheeks, and burned away the fog, but she couldn't stop shivering. Her clothes clung to her and felt like icepacks.

"I need dry clothes," she gasped. "Or I need to dry these clothes."

She stood up, almost banging her head on the overhang. With no thought of modesty, she threw her windbreaker, jeans, cardigan, t-shirt, shoes, underwear, and socks in a damp pile beside the fire. Soon she was wrapped in her blanket, wilting towards the heat.

The waves rumbled and crashed.

As she stared into the flames, the fog drew closer. Her vision blurred, and she tried to shake it clear. I mustn't sleep, she thought. Worst thing to do if you have hypothermia. Just stay close to the bonfire ... and remember.

"Yum," said Peter. "It's just like caramel!"

She looked up. Red-gold flames licked away the fog. As she watched, the bay came into focus. She could see an arm of the escarpment reaching out into the water, bathed orange in the setting sun. Peter held a stick away from the bonfire, licking his fingers.

Rosemary laughed. "As if you wouldn't believe me." She squished her marshmallow between two graham crackers and pulled it off the stick. "You never roasted marshmallows? Ever?" She set her stick down and rubbed her hand on her jeans.

"Never. Can I have another?"

She rummaged through her knapsack. "We're almost out," she said.

"How?" asked Peter. "We bought a whole package!"

She gave him a playful scowl. "You lost half of it in the flames."

"Told you I never did this before," said Peter. "I need practice. We should have bought two packages."

"You'll make do." She bit into her s'more.

Her teeth clicked on nothing.

Rosemary shook her head so hard, it rattled. The image of Peter faded into the fog until she was sitting by herself. Her blanket fluttered in the cold wind. The breakers roared.

"What ... the hell?" she gasped.

Then the sea-woman's words echoed in her head: "*This place echoes memories. Don't be ensnared.*"

Memories. Like shipwrecks, played out over and over again? Like *her* memories?

It had been so real. She could still taste the memory of marshmallows and graham crackers. Already she could feel things circling around her. She saw flashes at the edge of her vision like multi-coloured cobwebs.

She stood up with a shout, and the memories scampered away with the fog. She leaned against the rocks, breathing heavily. Then she picked up her underwear and rubbed it between her fingers. It was dry.

Later, warm and dressed, Rosemary stepped away from a broken container at the waterline, opening a keyed can of preserved meat. She wrinkled her nose, but dug in her fingers and nibbled at the pasty contents. Beside her, the bonfire waned.

Okay, she thought. That's one crisis dealt with. Now what do I do?

Look for Peter, obviously.

How? she wondered. How do you search when you don't even know where you are?

She looked up and down the beach again, up to where it vanished in the fog. Her eyes fell on the broken cargo containers. Curiosity twigged, and she stepped forward for a better look.

Picking up a fallen plank, she stared at the letters printed across it. It read: "USS *Lorelei*."

She blinked. "That was over a hundred and eighty years ago!"

This box had been the one with the food.

"Ugh!" She cast the container aside, then picked it up again and stared at it. The tin gleamed in the twilight as though it had been made months ago, not centuries. The meat did not smell appetizing, but it didn't smell rancid, either.

Moving to another container, she shoved some broken pieces of wood aside and opened up one of the smaller boxes within. Her eyes widened. The boxes contained nails: old iron nails of the sort made before mass production, as shiny as the day they were made.

Cargo containers smashed against the rocks, but showing no other signs of decay; food that should have been rotten but was edible (she hoped).

"Well, Toto, we're not in Clarksbury anymore," she said.

Then her eyes fell upon another container further out in the water. Glass was scattered over the protruding stones. They were the remains of bottles, of a sort that Rosemary had only seen in the antiques market. Some of the bottles weren't broken.

She hopped from rock to rock, keeping an eye out for broken glass underfoot, and picked up one of the unbroken bottles. It was filled with a white liquid. "Milk? Well, here's a test." The lid was made of foil, and she peeled it off using her fingers and her teeth. She sniffed the contents, then took a tentative sip, then gulped it down and stared at the empty bottle. "I'm standing in the middle of the best refrigerator ever made!"

She tossed the bottle back inside the cargo container with a clink. "Neat. Now what do I do?"

Go find Peter, she thought.

"Where?" she muttered.

I don't know, but I've found all I can in this spot. It's time to go somewhere else.

"Let's take along some supplies."

She wrapped some matches and some cans of food and Sterno in her blanket and stuck one of the bottles of milk in her pocket. Turning to douse the bonfire, she stopped and noticed, for the first time, the thick black smoke that curled from it, up the cliff face and into the sky.

"Hmm." She stuck out her lip. "Here I am. Come and get me."

What an odd thought. Other than that sea-woman, I haven't seen a living thing since I got here.

A splash brought Rosemary's attention around.

The waves were a distant rumble, overpowered by the gentle lapping against the stones nearby. The sound was small and close by, like a pebble disturbed by a shifting foot.

Rosemary looked. In a still area of the cove, ripples reached out along the surface of the water. She could see nothing that could have caused them.

There was another splash, to Rosemary's left. Another set of ripples, closer, fanning out against the shore.

Rosemary backed away.

Another splash, another ripple. This time, she caught a glimpse of a small, black shape as it slipped back into the water.

Then something flew at her.

She swung up her pack instinctively. Something bounced off it and fell with a splat onto the rocks.

Rosemary lowered her pack and stared.

The creature was an eel with legs and a tail, covered in scales that glistened with water. It had a huge unhinged jaw with many long and pointed teeth.

It rounded on her with the speed of a salamander when she dared take a closer look. It opened its jaw and let out a venomous hiss.

Rosemary scrambled back, barely taking it all in. What was this creature? Was it a fish?

There was another splash, and then another.

Rosemary had a nasty thought: fish sometimes travel in schools.

Something leapt at her out of the murk. Rosemary screamed and swung her pack. A long-tailed shape sailed out past a far tide pool.

She only just saw the other shape out of the corner of her eye when it sank its teeth into her forearm. She cried out and swung it against a rock again and again. The creature squealed, but it did not let go, even when it stopped moving.

Other shapes leapt forward and Rosemary ran for her life. Behind her, the sound of splashes became like applause, growing to an ovation that paced her along the shoreline.

CHAPTER SIX
ARIEL

"Breathe, Peter."

Peter floundered, struggling for air and light.

He felt himself sinking, pulled deeper and deeper by song. He reached for the shimmering ceiling above him, but darkness swept over his vision. It pressed.

Music rang in his ears: a haunting, lilting tune that came into his ears with the water. He wanted it in his lungs. He wanted to breathe.

Even though it would kill him.

He wanted to breathe in, water and song. His chest convulsed. He flailed desperately, but silky strands wrapped around him and held him still. The song broke off. "Easy, Peter. Relax. Breathe."

The water slipped into his mouth and into his nose. Finally, he could resist no longer. The water swept into him.

"Breathe," said Fiona.

Peter opened his eyes. He was floating in aquamarine, the shimmering surface within arms reach.
Fiona stood above him, her hair fluttering in the cur-
rent, her arms beneath his back. She smiled down at
him. "Peter?" He wasn't sure if he heard her words
with his ears or his mind.

"Am I in heaven?" he found himself asking, surpris-
ingly calm.

Fiona laughed like a flute underwater. "No."

"Are you sure?" He wasn't sure if he was speaking,
or how Fiona heard him.

"Certain."

"Then, where am I?"

"Home." She hauled him to the surface. "Breathe!"

Peter burst from the surface, gasping. The sweetest
air filled his lungs. He coughed and flailed, weak with
relief. Fiona held him as he sagged into her.

"Thanks," he wheezed. He shook his head, trying
to clear it, and gazed around blearily.

I thought I was dead. Why did I think I was dead?

Falling ... Rosemary ... their screams mingling ...
the lake rushing up ...

He flailed, raising spray.

"Rosemary! Rosemary, where are you?"

Fiona grabbed at him. "Peter, calm yourself! You're
safe, now."

"No! Rosemary!" His voice echoed.

Fiona touched his brow and caught him as he went limp in her arms. She sat him down in the shallow water. "Rest," she whispered. She cupped her hand into the lake and brought the water to his lips. "Drink."

Peter swallowed the sweet water. It settled into his chest like a cool pebble. His ragged breathing eased. Tension slipped from his shoulders along with the fears from his mind.

Fiona smiled. "Yes."

Peter let out the breath he was holding. "Where am I?" he whispered.

"Home. Look." She helped him back to his feet.

Peter opened his eyes, then closed them immediately as the world swam around him. Fiona held him steady until he was ready to look again.

He stood knee deep in water a few feet from shore. The breeze blew at his back, warm as a hair dryer. A line of cliffs rose around them, topped by trees of green, red, and gold. A line of flowerpot islands — small columns of stone — stretched out into the bay.

As his gaze reached the sky, he frowned. There were no clouds. No sun or stars, either. The dome above was a smooth aquamarine. "That can't be right," he muttered. The cliffs were no different from those around Clarksbury. Even the water tasted the same, and yet ... where *was* he?

And how did he get here?

Fiona pressed his back, gently. "Can you walk?"

He swallowed. "Yeah." They splashed ashore. Peter stood dripping. Fiona looked dry. They stood a moment, staring at each other. Fiona smiled at him. Her hair fluttered in the breeze. The waves slapped the shore. Finally, Peter broke the silence. "So ... where do we go now?"

"I told you," said Fiona, kindly. "Home."

"How do we get there?"

"We follow that girl." Fiona pointed. Peter looked. Behind him, on the top of one of a boulder that stood at the water's edge, sat a young girl, no more than nine. She had brown curls, wore green robes, and sat facing the bay, knees hugged to her chest.

"Ariel!" Fiona called, and the girl perked up. She looked at them and, at the sight of Fiona, squealed and scrambled down the face of the rock. She ran into Fiona's arms. "Fionarra! You're back!"

Fiona embraced her. "Ariel."

Peter frowned at her. "Fionarra?"

She smiled ruefully. "You may call me Fiona."

Ariel squirmed free of Fiona's embrace and turned to Peter. She stopped when she looked up at him. She swallowed. "Is this ... him?"

"Yes, Ariel, this is Peter."

Peter shifted under Ariel's gaze of awe. The stones clicked beneath his feet. "Er ... hi!"

Ariel squeaked and ducked behind Fiona. Peter blushed.

Fiona stepped aside and pushed Ariel into the open. "Don't be shy. You've so wanted to meet Peter."

Peter swallowed hard. "Hi," he said again.

"Hello," said the girl.

The waves lapped the beach. Peter and Ariel stared at each other, unsure what to say. He'd never seen her before, he was sure, but there was something familiar about that round face, the brown hair, and the wide brown eyes.

Then Fiona pushed them forward. "Come, you two. The village awaits."

Peter felt his stomach drop. "Village?"

"And your family," said Fiona.

Family. The word knotted his stomach. This place was at once familiar and not familiar. The shape of the bay, Ariel. His future filled him with hope and dread. It pressed at him like the water and song. He kept himself from taking Fiona's hand, and followed her.

As they walked, Ariel forgot her shyness. She bounded ahead and back, chattering. Her curls bobbed as she bombarded him with questions.

"Did you live in a house back where you were?" asked Ariel. "With electricity?"

"Um ... yeah." Peter gave Fiona a look, but she just smiled.

"And cars? Did you have a car?"

"Uh ... yes."

"Were you lonely?"

Peter blinked at her and glanced at Fiona.

Ariel went squealing after some sandpipers and Peter couldn't help but grin. "Is she your sister?"

Fiona shook her head, but she didn't meet his gaze.

They followed the beach to where the cliffs bowed low. As they started to ascend, Peter stopped and turned back.

"Wait a minute ..."

The shape of the bay, the path they were on, were almost like what he remembered of the shoreline near Clarksbury. Almost ...

As he stared back at the bay, he could see the escarpment stretching out into the water, but on his left when it should be on his right. The shape of the bay was mirror-image to what he was used to.

"It's ... backwards."

Fiona pulled at his sleeve. "Your people are waiting."

The knot returned to Peter's stomach, but he followed her. The continuing clash between déjà vu and the strangeness of the world didn't help. The first trees he saw were Earth trees (apples, maples, and aspen), but in all the seasons of the year (seeds, flowers, and fruit). Some leaves were turning red and gold, and other leaves were just coming out.

Someone had nailed a bucket to a maple and was collecting sap.

Then they turned onto the shelf that stretched back from the top of the escarpment, and Peter saw the village.

Ariel pointed ahead of them. "That's where I live!"

The pathway led to a central park, bounded by houses on all sides. The park was a large patch of grass with a copse of trees at one side, and a small amphitheatre of stones in the middle, like a dry wading pool. Familiarity welled up in Peter's stomach and lodged as a lump in his throat.

The surrounding homes were tall and thin, ragged-topped as if with gables, made of smooth stone the colour of brick. Behind the houses, a line of cliffs rose up like distant skyscrapers.

And people. Women passed with long hair fluttering behind them; men sat in doorways and talked. Their clothes were odd — green or blue tunics with hose — but the familiarity remained. Their friendly, neighbourhood chatter reached out to him across years.

It was all Peter could do to not run into the third house down the street, calling for his mom. Instead, he stood at the entrance to the park, until the sirens called to them.

"Fionarra!" people shouted. "Welcome back!"

Ariel waved and Fiona smiled. She touched Peter's back and gently, but firmly, pushed him forward towards the third house down the street. His, after all. His home.

Conversations stopped when Peter and Fiona passed by, then started again as whispers.

"It's him, isn't it?"

Peter suddenly felt the eyes of the whole village on him, from every person outside and from every window. Ariel led him by the hand, across a gravel road and over a stone walk and a patch of green stones like a lawn, towards the steps leading to a small porch. "Home!" she said. The front door was open for them. Peter hesitated, but felt the eyes all on his back. He swallowed once, then stepped inside.

"The Lost Child, come home!" said Fiona, at his back.

In a tall, narrow foyer, he stood on floorboards, amongst walls that were a smooth, beige stone. Ariel darted into the hallway with a shriek of laughter, her bare feet slapping. Peter listened to the sound like an echo.

"Take off your coat," said Fiona, stepping back.

Peter took off his windbreaker and, without thinking, tossed it at the wall. It caught neatly on a hook and hung by its collar. Peter stood a moment, arm outstretched in the act of throwing, staring at his jacket.

Then he heard Ariel's voice echoing from the kitchen. "Everybody! Fionarra's home and she's brought the Lost One with her!"

There was a burst of talk and chairs scraping back.

Peter took a backwards step towards the door.

Fiona touched his shoulder. "Peter? What's wrong?"

Peter struggled to keep his breath. "Fiona, I'm not ready."

Fiona frowned. "What are you —"

"I-I can't deal with this ... it's too much." He pushed back against Fiona's gently restraining arm. What if he didn't know his family? What if he didn't like them? What if they didn't like him? What if he wasn't really home? "I-I'm not ready."

Fiona's hand moved from his shoulder to his temple. "Peter, please come."

His doubts vanished. He followed down the hall and into the kitchen. The walls and floors felt uneven, though they looked level. He was reminded of a sea cave furnished at yard sales. There was a church pew along one wall. A hat stand with a missing arm. They passed a room where Peter could see a cupboard with blue paint peeling. The television and his toys would be inside that. A basket of magazines and a folded quilt. Or ... not.

Suddenly there was a crowd of people, Ariel bobbing among them. It was as if she'd created them while he'd been lost inside the memory of his parents' TV cupboard. Suddenly he was the centre of attention. People embraced, poked, and prodded until he felt like a plush toy.

"So," said a tall woman standing apart from the crowd. She had Fiona's hair and slim build, but there were crow's feet under her eyes, and wrinkles over the line of her jaw. "This is young Peter, come back to us?"

"Yes, Mother," said Fiona, pushing him forward proudly. "On the other side, he was known as Peter McAllister."

Fiona's mother put a hand on Peter's shoulder. "Then that name you shall retain, unless you choose otherwise. I am Eleanna. Welcome back to our world."

Peter mouth was dry. "Thank you," he stammered. "It's ... er ... good to be here."

"Come to the kitchen. You must be hungry after your long journey. Please, eat."

They led him into a room with a hearth in the corner. There was a basin cut into a stone shelf. A big butcher's block stood like an altar at the middle of the room. The air smelled like a feast and there was food everywhere.

Eleanna pressed a small, round, reddish-brown cake into Peter's hands before he had a chance to refuse. It was warm and smelled of fish. He took a bite, more to avoid offence than out of hunger. More food was pressed into his hands.

You shouldn't eat the food of the dead, said some stray part of his memory.

"It is good to have you come back to us, Peter McAllister," said a tall woman with waist-length black hair. "It has been too long since we have had a Homecoming."

"Homecoming?" Peter repeated.

"How was your journey?"

"What is it like on the other side?"

The chatter began to fly.

"Do they still light their homes with electricity, or have they found something else?"

"Why do they make their boats so noisy?"

"Were you lonely?"

Peter felt as if the attention was pressing on him. He thought he might drown. He grabbed at the altar for help.

A tall man with a red beard leaned close. "How was your journey?" Peter could feel the man's voice in his chest. He was huge.

"I-I-I don't remember." He felt short of breath. More plates were pressed close.

The tall man frowned at Fiona. "How came you to find him, Fionarra?"

She stared back coolly. "Though hard work and perseverance, Merius."

Merius picked up a trident that had been set by the kitchen door, and left the room.

Still the chatter continued. And with it, other questions bombarded Peter's mind. Who are all these people? What's missing? Who's missing? Where's Rosemary?

Sweat trickled down Peter's brow. He swayed, dizzy.

Fiona stepped through the crowd. Her hand clamped on Peter's shoulder, and his thoughts vanished. "Please," she said to the others, "Peter has had a long journey. We should give him time to rest." She took Peter by the arm. The kitchen was much quieter, suddenly, as if half the people had vanished. "Come, Peter. Let's find you a room."

"Wait!" Peter shook her off. "Where are they? Where are my parents?"

A silence fell upon the kitchen. It filled Peter's heart with lead.

"Come on," he said. "You said I'd find my family here, so where are they? Where are my parents?"

Eleanna shifted uncomfortably. "Peter, I'm sorry —"

The ground slipped from Peter's feet. "No!"

He was running by the time he got to the kitchen door.

"Peter!" Fiona cried.

He darted into the hallway, hearing people call his name. He ran for … where? But he knew he had to find someplace where he could be alone. He'd been alone for six years, and then he wasn't, and then he was again. The family he never knew was already gone.

He dashed for the front door, skidding to a halt as it opened before another visitor. He ducked into a room and hid in a corner.

He stood in the hollow behind the door as people milled about in the hallway. Some went out the front door, calling his name. Others returned to the kitchen, speaking in hushed tones. Finally, everyone was gone.

"Peter?"

Except for Ariel, who seemed exceptionally good at hide and seek.

She stood in front of him, eyes wide with curiosity. "Why did you run away?"

He took a deep breath to answer, then stopped. "You wouldn't understand."

"Fionarra says you are tired."

He sighed. "Yes. No. Coming here ... it's a shock, a big shock. And then ..."

"Then, what?"

"I ... I've been alone for so long. I came to find my family."

"But you have a family, now! The village is a family."

"A village isn't a family," snapped Peter. "Don't you get it? My parents ... my parents died. I didn't have anybody at home. And now I come here, and you tell me my parents died here again? I mean, what are the odds? It's like a curse or something. What happened to them?"

Ariel shifted uncomfortably. "They just ... died."

He knelt in front of her. "You knew them? How did they die?"

She bit her lip. "It was their time."

"What do you —" He stopped when he saw a tear brim and trickle down her cheek. "What ... are you crying?"

"Mom and Dad!" Ariel said, and she hugged him, sobbing on his shoulder.

"Wha—" Peter mouthed. Then he pried Ariel's arms off of him and held her by her shoulders. She cleared her nose with a sniff. "Were they your parents, too?"

She nodded.

He blinked. "You're my sister?"

She sucked her lip, then nodded.

"You're my *sister*?"

She nodded again.

"Why didn't you tell me?"

"I ... I couldn't."

Peter had to sit down, now. There were no chairs, so he made do with the floor.

"You're my sister," he repeated. "Oh my god."

"Peter?"

"What do I do now? I-I-I didn't even know I *had* a sister!"

"Just be my brother," she said. "Be with me. I have nobody to be with."

"Ariel ...." Peter shifted the unfamiliar name over his tongue. "I can't just ... I can't —"

"Why not?"

"I just can't!"

Ariel stared at him. Her eyes glistened. "Don't you *want* a sister, Peter?"

He stared in horror at her tears. "I ... come here." He drew her into a tight hug. She was warm and soft — not sea-glass smooth like Fiona, just little-kid soft. Human. Real. His sister. "I'm sorry. I just ... there are so many changes. I was scared."

"You must have been so lonely," Ariel whispered into his shoulder.

"You have no idea." He squeezed her. It was the happiest moment of his life. And he was crying.

A part of his mind spoke up, whispering *"where's Rosemary?"* into his thoughts. It went ignored. He held Ariel close.

CHAPTER SEVEN
SOMETHING RICH AND STRANGE

Rosemary kept running long after the splashing pursuit faded behind her. It was only when she stumbled, barking her shins on the stones, that her body took over and told her to rest.

She lay gasping for breath. If she had wanted any proof she wasn't in Clarksbury anymore, she had it. Unless Bruce Nuclear had had an accident, Georgian Bay was not populated by flying salamander piranhas.

As her heart slowed, her forearm started throbbing. The dead piranha was still hanging there, teeth buried deep under her skin. Rosemary worked her fingers into the creature's mouth and forced the jaws apart with a wet snap. Blood trickled down her wrist and off her fingers in rivulets. Now she had time to think about it, it hurt. A lot.

Cupping water in her left hand, she washed the blood off her other arm. She pulled off her scarf and wrapped it around the wound, using her teeth to cinch it tight. She flexed her fingers, and gasped at the bolt of pain.

Every profanity she knew went through her mind, and she resolved to learn more. Slumping against a boulder, she caught the rest of her breath.

Another shipwreck in the fog; the gunnels of a steamship poked above the waves. Wooden furniture of the sort Rosemary hadn't seen outside of an antique shop lay scattered about. There was no sign of any people.

"This is a graveyard," she muttered.

She swallowed. Then she pushed on, wondering what to do next.

"The flying piranhas change nothing," she said to the air. "I have to find Peter, and I won't leave until I do."

No, the flying piranhas change everything. I'm not alone on this world, and the creatures that are here want to eat me.

"I just need to avoid the water."

I was hoping to get across that water. The only boats I've found are wrecked. What do I do? Grab some planks and nails and build myself a raft?

"Something will come up. Just keep moving."

The stones clattered beneath her, a sound of slow rockslides. The breakers rumbled at the edge of hearing. As she pressed forward, the familiar sounds washed over her. Stones beneath her feet. Waves breaking on the shore. If it were just a little warmer, it would have been just like the time when she and Peter ...

No. Stop. Focus. Forward.

A wave rolled in and splashed her feet. She burst out laughing.

Ahead of her, Peter stumbled backwards, and squeezed the water from his pant leg. "Hey!" he shouted. "I've got to walk home in these pants!"

"They'll dry, silly!" she said. She pushed past him and ran for the water's edge, barefoot. She ducked back as a wave rolled in, soaking her calves up to her knees. She let out a shriek. "Cold!"

"Serves you right!" Peter yelled. But he was smiling.

"Come on, Peter!" said Rosemary. "It's fun!"

"Uh uh!" said Peter, shaking his head vehemently. "No swimsuit, no water!"

"Don't be lame, Peter!" She threw water at him. "Loosen up —" Her words cut off with a scream as a breaker struck the back of her legs, sending her sprawling into the surf.

"Rosemary!" Peter rushed into the water. As he reached for her, she grabbed his wrist and pulled. Peter's yell ended with a glub as he went into the drink. He surged to the surface. "You did that on purpose!"

"Yeah," said Rosemary. "Just like this." And she pushed him in again.

He came out, gasping. "You're mean!"

"I can't help it." She held out her hand. "Here."

"Thanks," he said, and pulled her under.

They splashed until the chill sent them onto dry land.

They sat dripping, on the stones, basking in the warm air as twilight deepened. Rosemary settled back with a contented sigh.

"This is perfect," said Peter.

"Yes, it is," she replied.

But I'm forgetting something, she thought.

"What?" she muttered.

Peter.

She opened her eyes, and blinked at the starless navy-blue sky. "Peter?"

"Hmm?" said his voice beside her.

"Oh, nothing."

That's not him.

"Course it's him, silly." She closed her eyes and began to drift off.

No, it's not. It was him, but now it's just a memory of him.

"Huh?"

Get up.

"What's wrong?" he said.

"I ...." She frowned. "I need to be somewhere."

"Where?"

You need to keep looking for Peter.

"But he's right here," she mumbled.

Peter laughed. "You're not making sense."

That's because this doesn't make sense. Peter's gone! They kidnapped him! You've got to go and find him!

"What?" she mumbled. She shook her head clear. "I'm looking for something," she said. "I have to keep looking."

"Did you lose something?" asked Peter.

"Yes." Her brow furrowed. "I have to keep looking." She pushed herself to her feet, and picked up her knapsack.

He looked up at her. "You're leaving?"

"I've got to." But her feet wouldn't move.

"I'll help you," said Peter. He touched her shoulder. "But stay a bit." He nodded. "Look at what the sunset's doing."

The base of the escarpment reaching out into the bay was dark, but the top and its trees glowed bright orange against the darkening sky. "It's beautiful."

"Yeah." She sat down. "Yeah, it's beautiful." Unconsciously, she snuggled closer to him. He put an arm around her. "Just a few minutes, then I've got to go."

"Okay," he said.

And as she watched the sunset play against the top of the escarpment, she lost track of time.

The waves rumbled.

Gradually, she became aware of a vibration in her body; like standing next to a big speaker at a dance. A bass note hummed in her chest. She found herself flicking her hand past her ear, as if to brush away an annoying mosquito, and realized that the low note had been joined by another of higher pitch.

Then she realized the sounds were no hallucination.

She sat up. Peter vanished in a burst of fog. She looked longingly at the space where he'd been, and then clarity set in with a thunderclap. She was not in Clarksbury anymore. She was in deadly danger. And something had woken her up from her dream.

She scrambled to her feet. Her clothes were dripping. She could feel their cold biting into her skin, but she scrambled behind the cover of a rock. She could see the fog pulling back. The rock face and water were solidifying like ice melting backwards. She pulled her knapsack beside her as she scanned the land and water. Finally, she caught a flicker of motion beyond the waves.

She focussed on that speck as it grew larger, until it revealed itself as a boat. It was small and thin and moved without sail or oars or noise, cutting through waves it had no business cutting through. Two people were on board: a woman at the prow and a man at the stern, holding the rudder.

The two had their mouths open, and the double-note song was coming from them. The difference in their size matched the difference in their pitch. The woman looked as thin as a pole, and the man was three times her size. Neither stopped to take a breath until the boat neared shore. The singing stopped when the boat crunched onto the stones.

Rosemary watched from behind the cover of the large rock. The woman's red hair stretched beyond the small of her back. The man bore a thick black beard. Both had skin like weathered glass, eyes like coals, and webbing between their fingers.

Just like the woman who had pulled Peter into this world, Rosemary thought. Maybe they know where Peter has been taken. Maybe they'll help.

They pulled a pair of harpoons out of the boat.

Or maybe not.

As she watched, the couple glanced warily at the small cove beyond her rock. They turned to each other, joined hands, and began to chant.

As with their singing, the sounds were barely audible to the human ear, but they tugged at Rosemary's heart and shook her brain. She felt sick, but she kept listening.

The chants quickened, and the couple pulled apart, leaving two people in the space between them.

Rosemary gasped. Where there had been two, now there were four. A second man and a second woman stood, clasping hands. The man was slimmer than the first and wore a red beard, while the woman had black hair and was huskier than her counterpart. Both had harpoons already in their hands.

They turned to face the rock. For a frightening moment, Rosemary thought these four might be hunting her. Why else would they land here, harpoons at the ready?

But from the way the four concentrated on the cove beyond the rock, Rosemary realized that she wasn't what they were after.

She frowned. If they weren't after her, then what were they here for?

Behind her, the fog erupted into a mass of tentacles. A giant squid rose out from a cove, roaring. Rosemary dove for cover as the four figures rushed the water, stabbing and slashing. The battle was short and brutal. Finally, the squid thrashed and fell limp. The hunters stared at their kill in triumph.

Leaving the bulky man and his second to tie ropes to the squid's tentacles, the two women returned to the boat. Along the way, they stopped by the shipwreck and eyed a richly carved, dark wooden bench. They chattered to each other, gesturing from the bench to the boat, their voices barely carrying across the stones. Each grabbed an end and hefted it over the stones.

Rosemary brushed wet hair from her eyes, and watched the women work. As she circled around the rock to keep them in sight, her feet slipped. Stones clattered. The women looked up.

"Darius?" asked the red-haired woman. "Is that you?"

Rosemary crouched lower.

The red-haired woman set the bench down. "Why are you hiding behind that rock? We have work to do!"

There was now nothing to lose. Rosemary stepped out of hiding and tried to look ... friendly. Confident. Not scared to her toes.

"Hey," she called.

The red-haired woman stumbled back with a gasp. Her black-haired cousin disappeared without so much as a puff of smoke.

Rosemary stared at the spot where the dark-haired woman had stood, then shook the questions out of her head. "Hey," she said again.

The woman stared at Rosemary in horror.

Rosemary raised her hands, palms out, wondering how she could possibly make herself look less threatening. "I didn't mean to startle you," she said carefully. "I'm not going to hurt you. I need your help."

The shock faded from the woman's face, replaced by a wary glare.

"Please," said Rosemary. "I need someone to take me across the water. Can you do that?"

The woman's wariness intensified. "Darius!" She hardly raised her voice, but the tone of it cut across the stones and stung Rosemary's ears. "Darius! Come quickly!"

"Loria!" The thick-set man came running, his second nowhere to be seen. "What is it? Why did you cut your song?" He stopped short at the sight of Rosemary. "Who is this?"

Before Rosemary could say anything, Loria cut in. "She broke my song! She broke it with her words!"

Darius stepped protectively in front of Loria. "What is the meaning of this?" he snarled at Rosemary. "Who are you?"

"M-my name is R-rosemary," she stammered. "I-I'm not here to hurt you or anything. I just need —"

She halted when Darius raised his harpoon. "Stay back, songbreaker!" Glaring at Rosemary, Darius hustled Loria to the boat.

"What about our kill?" Loria protested.

"We'll hunt another day," said Darius. "We must warn our village. Go!"

"Wait!" Rosemary stood, flabbergasted, as the two pushed off from shore. They sped across the waves, briefly interrupting their song to flash her looks of hostility and fear.

She began to shiver in the wind again. The fog returned, rolling across the water towards her.

***

When Fiona found Peter, his tears were still dripping into Ariel's hair. Fiona stood by the door, her gaze cast down in shame. "Peter, I am so sorry. I should have told you everything before I brought you here. I made a mistake."

"It's okay." Peter let go of Ariel, dried his eyes, and stood up. "I'm ready to meet everyone, now."

"They've all gone home."

"Everyone?"

"Everyone except my mother, of course. This is her home."

"Then I'll start with her."

Fiona put a hand on his shoulder. "Only if you are ready, Peter. Do not push yourself."

"If I wait until I'm ready, I'll never meet anyone. Let's go meet our family." Ariel caught at his hand.

The house was silent, save for a few subdued voices in the kitchen. Peter hesitated at the threshold, but forced himself forward. Eleanna was sitting on a stool beside the butcher's block, talking to a strikingly tall and dark-haired woman. At Peter's entrance, the woman stood, hugged Fiona's mother, and left.

Peter stood across the butcher's block from Eleanna, silent and uncertain. The old woman indicated other stools. "Please, sit down, all of you." Her voice was as warm as the Gulf Stream. Peter, Fiona, and Ariel took their places at once.

There was another uncomfortable silence as the four stared at each other. Peter tried to work up the courage to say something, but Eleanna beat him to it. "Welcome to our home, Peter McAllister."

"Thank you, Mrs...." Peter hesitated, suddenly realizing he'd never known Fiona's last name. "I'm sorry, but what should I call you?"

Eleanna blinked and smiled. "Ah, yes, the human custom of multiple names. Do forgive me. I haven't much experience with introductions. My name is just Eleanna, so Eleanna will do."

"It's good to meet you." Peter looked at the table. "I'm sorry I bolted just now."

"No need to be sorry," said Eleanna. "I understand how you must feel. I also understand that there are several questions you want to ask. Ask them. I'll answer."

Peter swallowed. "How did my birth parents die?"

Fiona reached for him. "Peter, are you sure —"

"Just tell me, please!"

"It was their time," said Eleanna.

"You mean they died of old age? But, I'm only sixteen, Ariel's barely ...." Five? Ten? He had no idea, he found. She was a little kid but she seemed old, too. Then again, people said that about him: sixteen going on forty. "I'm not old enough to have parents die of old age."

"I told you that we were not human, Peter," Fiona cut in. "We are built differently, as is our world. Our lives are long and full, but we pass quickly."

Peter mulled over this answer until he was satisfied with it. He nodded. Now for his other big question. "Why did you leave me ... over there?"

Fiona touched his shoulder. Her mother took a deep breath, but couldn't answer.

"Because there are so few of us," said Ariel. "There are only one hundred and fifty-seven people in this village."

"A hundred and fifty-seven?" said Peter. "What about the other villages?"

"There are no other villages," said Ariel.

Eleanna took Peter's hand. "Let me be honest, Peter. Our people are dying. Rather than doom the few who remain to a dwindling life, we give our children to humanity ... when we can. They live their whole lives as human, and take what joy they can."

"Then why am I back here?"

"Because of Ariel," said Eleanna.

"Those of us sent to live with humans are solitary, lonely people," said Fiona. "Because you were orphaned, your suffering was much worse. And your sister was here, the only siren child, lonely too. We decided that we had to bring you two together."

Peter caught Ariel looking at him from behind a screen of curls. He smiled at her. A big-brother smile. It felt good.

"You see," said Eleanna, as if reading his mind. "It is right that you are together, now."

* * *

Peter felt better after dinner. The food was tasty and filling, and it took all of his resistance to keep Fiona's mother from stuffing him with third and fourth helpings. In the end, he sat at the table, nursing a steaming mug of tea and smiling as Ariel amused herself with a porcelain doll, and Fiona and Eleanna discussed village politics.

Then Ariel began to yawn. She caught Peter looking, smiled sheepishly, and returned to playing, but her eyes drooped. Chuckling, Peter nudged Fiona, and nodded to Ariel.

Eleanna stood up. "Perhaps it is time, Peter, to put Ariel to bed."

Peter picked Ariel up and carried her as she sagged onto his shoulder. He followed Fiona through the halls, past a room scattered with toys including a metal jack-in-the-box and a clockwork train, past a bathroom with a large basin cut into stone with a bucket of water waiting for a bath, to a closed door, solid oak, with shiny brass fittings. Fiona opened it onto a neat bedroom, with pink stone walls and a small wooden-frame bed draped with lace covers.

Ariel was asleep in Peter's arms. He juggled her carefully, pulled down the covers, and set her on the mattress, prying her arms from around his neck. She settled into her pillows, her breathing deep and regular, smiling. Peter stood up and stared at Ariel in awe.

This is too good to be true, he thought.

Fiona touched his shoulder warmly, then led him to the door. Peter left, looking back.

Then the door swung closed between them, making no sound.

Peter blinked. The warmth inside him cooled. He looked at the walls and the doors with a new intensity. Something wasn't right. Questions bubbled at the back of his mind. Where was he? How did he get here?

"Peter?"

He started, and looked behind him. Fiona had opened another door and was beckoning him in. It was a small and cozy bedroom, with a window, a tall dark wooden closet with straight sides, and, beside that, a chest of light wooden drawers, full of curves. In the middle of the room, a canoe extended from the wall, its wooden struts removed and its insides filled with feature cushions draped over with a blanket. Peter wondered if it rocked like a cradle.

He couldn't help laughing. "What a house. I haven't seen a mix of styles like this outside of Rosemary's ..."

Fiona sucked her lips against her teeth.

He shuddered. Rosemary! How could he have forgotten ...

Fiona touched his shoulder, and the thought vanished from his mind. The emptiness echoed like a void.
He touched his forehead, and looked at her. Another
memory slipped into his mind, silent like the closing
door. "How did you find me?"

Her brow furrowed. She cocked her head.

The memory repeated. Sliding doors opening; a
gurney pushed through. A doctor's voice echoed in his
mind's eye. "Peter?"

"Peter?" Fiona's voice barged into his thoughts.

"Why ... why did it take so long?"

"What?"

"Six years." Peter shook his head. "What were you
do—"

Fiona grabbed him by the back of his neck and
pulled him into his room. She planted a firm kiss on his
lips, and caught him as his knees gave way.

"It did take time to find you," she said, pulling him
further into the room. "I almost gave up more than
once. But one thing kept me going."

"W-what?"

Fiona kicked the door closed. It clicked shut
behind them, isolating them from the rest of the house
as effectively as a moat. The gleam in her eye filled
Peter's consciousness. "You."

He struggled to think, but he couldn't look away. "W-what are you doing?" He caught the scent of her and had to breathe her in. She was like a breeze off the ocean. His heart beat like a Taiko drum.

She smiled. "What I know you've wanted from the very beginning."

He swooned, but she held him up. Then she kissed him, and all sense of time vanished. He pressed against her desperately.

She pulled away, smiling at the vacant look in his eyes. "Welcome home."

CHAPTER EIGHT
MERIUS

Rosemary looked at her watch. It was still broken.

She tore it from her wrist, grunting as she threw it at the waves.

The glass had smashed on her journey to this world. She didn't know if it was the fall, the wave, or any of her stumbles on the stony beach. Her legs were criss-crossed with cuts and bruises. Her bandaged arm jabbed her with pain every time she moved it, and once again she'd been soaked. She shivered on a rock by the roaring fire, wrapped in a blanket, her drying clothes spread out around her.

It could be worse, she told herself. My glasses could have been smashed instead of my watch. Then it wouldn't matter how foggy it was. And one thing: something about her encounter with the sea creatures had blasted a bolt of clarity through her brain. The fog and the memories they contained seemed to be holding back warily. She could see far out to the lake, and even caught glimpses of the navy blue sky. She tested the dampness of her bra.

She told herself again that it could be worse as she shrugged on her cardigan and zipped up her windbreaker, but then she gave up. It was impossible to tell time in this perpetual twilight. She'd stopped to eat once, so she must have been here for hours. Progress made on finding Peter? Zilch.

She had food enough for six meals; two days, assuming she dared sleep. This shipwreck had provided her with firewood but nothing else. Going back for more food and Sterno meant braving the salamander piranhas. Going forward meant God-knew-what.

There was still the gully. That way led to defeat, but where else could she turn?

Exhausted, out of options, she leaned on a boulder, too tired to cry.

A splash brought her out of her daze.

She tensed against the stones, peering around. She caught sight of ripples on the water, far out into the lake, but closing in on the shore. As they approached, the ripples grew in clarity. The air above the water blew the fog forward like a shockwave.

She groped behind her and pulled a plank from the bonfire. The end of it burned in the breeze. She planted her feet and took a deep breath.

Then a man rose from the water.

Rosemary stumbled back.

He was the vision of Neptune, almost seven feet tall, with sea-glass skin, shoulder-length hair, and a thick, red beard. His eyes glowed glossy-black and there were hints of fins along the crest of his calves and forearms. He even carried a trident that sparkled and gleamed without sunlight.

He stopped at the sight of Rosemary, holding her plank like a firebrand.

She stared back.

In a lightning gesture, he flicked up his trident. "Explain yourself!" His voice was deep.

Rosemary turned and ran.

The merman dropped his trident. "Wait! Come back!"

Rosemary didn't listen. The stones clattered and splashed as she charged over the rises and through tide pools. She ran full tilt, not stopping until the water erupted before her.

She caught sight of a translucent creature with the head, torso, and arms of a woman. Below its stomach, the features bled together until it merged with the surface of the water. Its blue teeth were pointed and its wild hair blinded Rosemary with spray. Its hands ended in fearsome claws.

Rosemary swung her flaming plank. It passed

through harmlessly, the flames vanishing with a hiss. The water-woman roared, and clamped a hand over Rosemary's face. Rosemary's scream sucked water into her lungs.

Then the creature blew a wind like cold fire in Rosemary's face. The girl blinked crystals from her eyes.

The creature pulled back, its hand breaking off. A new one grew in its place immediately. Rosemary stumbled back, trying to breathe and wondering why her lungs weren't working. She couldn't open her mouth. She felt her face, and her fingers slipped across something cold, wet, and hard.

Her eyes widened in horror. Her heart raced. Ice encased the lower half of her face. Her lungs begged for air.

Rosemary toppled onto the wet stones, floundering. The creature raised its claws for the kill.

The bearded man leapt before her, spearing the creature with his trident. The metal glowed red, and the creature screamed, vanishing in a puff of steam.

Rosemary kicked and punched as the man hauled her into the air, but her struggles were feeble. The world grew blurry and slipped into black.

She blinked tears out of her eyes and found herself standing next to Peter on a ledge overlooking a deep ravine. The wind plucked at the fringes of her dress. She watched as the falling zeppelins cracked against the railway bridge and crumbled. Their burning metal skeletons rained on the valley floor.

Puck was in there. He'd killed himself to save them. He ...

She slumped to the ground.

Peter caught her. "We've got to keep going."

She slapped at him. "Leave me alone!"

"We have to keep going," he said, his voice level, firm. "Because he said so. Puck ...." He stumbled, and took a deep breath. "You're the hero. He ... he did what he did so that you could go on."

"You go, then," she said, shoving him away. "Just leave me alone!"

"No!" he shouted. "Not here, not now, not ever! Being alone is the worst thing in the world and I'm not doing that to you. We're in this together, and we've got to work together if we want to get out! I'm not leaving this spot until you get that!"

She blinked the tears from her eyes, then shook her head. Fresh air, like a breeze off a lake, filled her senses. "You're wrong. I mean, you're right, but ... this isn't real."

Peter blinked at her, but said nothing. She slipped her wrists from his grip and stepped back. "I've got to keep going. Maybe I got dragged here, but I would have come anyway. You followed me into a crazy place to save me. Now it's my turn!"

Movement made her look up. A flaming piece of fabric, skin from the zeppelin, fluttered down at her. She planted her feet, took a deep breath, and struck at it as it came close. "No! Wake up! I will wake up!"

The flames dodged her fists and fluttered before her eyes. Suddenly she saw that the fire was the bonfire reflected in the eyes of the merman who held her. She still couldn't breathe. She swung a punch at his nose. She clawed at the ice encasing her face.

The man leaned close and breathed hard. A hot wind enveloped her. The ice over her mouth and nose melted. She choked and coughed up water.

He set her on the beach beside the bonfire, where she lay like a baby, coughing and gasping at the same time.

When she had regained her breath, the man spoke. "Have you recovered, child?"

Rosemary coughed the last droplets from her lungs. Then, still clutching her chest, she rolled onto her back and looked at him. "I'm sorry," she wheezed.

The man raised his bushy red eyebrows. "That's not what a rescuer expects to hear. Wherefore are you sorry, lass?"

"Because I thought you were going to kill me, just like everything else in this world. Instead, you saved me. Thank you." Another coughing spell overtook her and she fell back.

The man chuckled and helped her sit up. "This is a dangerous place to those who don't know where the dangers lie."

Rosemary let out a sardonic laugh. "Yeah, I got that."

The man patted her on the back. "I like your temperament, lass. You are made of stern stuff. What be your name?"

"Rosemary. Rosemary Watson."

The man clasped her hand in his. His fingers extended past her wrist. "Welcome, Rosemary Watson. You may call me Merius."

He turned her hand over, revealing the blue-black birthmark in the centre of her palm. "Ah! I knew you were special. You have a mark."

"A mark?"

"On your palm. Such marks carry great significance among my people."

"This?" Rosemary held up her palm. "This isn't a birthmark, it's a ... yes. Great significance. I'm very significant. Yes."

Merius chuckled again. "Worry not, Rosemary. I would have rescued you, mark or no."

"That's great," said Rosemary. "Wonderful."

Relief swept through her. After hours on edge, fearing for her life, the lightness of her soul made her swoon. She lay before the bonfire and closed her eyes.

Merius said nothing, but crouched down and stared out on guard over the water.

Rosemary lay in a daze, collecting her thoughts. The wind whistled and the surf roared. Finally, with her eyes still closed, she said, "I need your help, Merius."

"I thought as much. How came you to be here?"

Rosemary opened one eye. The right side of her body was hot from the fire; her left side still wanted to shiver. "I fell off a cliff."

Merius raised his eyebrows. "How?"

"I was trying to keep a friend from falling off."

Merius stared at her. The flames of the bonfire reflected off his eyes. "You did not come alone?"

"No. I've been looking for my friend ever since. His name's Peter. Have you seen him?"

Merius looked away, deep in thought. Rosemary sat bolt upright. "You *have* seen him!"

"She said she brought him here alone," Merius muttered.

"Brought him here?" she echoed, her voice rising. "You know about this? Who kidnapped him? What do these people want from him? Who are they?"

"These people are my friends and my family," said Merius, not looking at her. "They are the people of my village."

Rosemary shifted away from him. "You approve of this?"

"I've seen it happen," said Merius. "A long time ago. But never with a second person complicating things."

"Complicating things?!"

"Yes. So, I have to ask, who is this Peter?" He looked at her. "What does he mean to you?"

"He's my friend." Rosemary stared as Merius's gaze darkened. "What's wrong?"

"How much of a friend?"

"A good friend! I went off a cliff for him? That sort of friend!"

"This is important!" Merius grabbed her by her shoulders, ignoring her squeak of fear. "How well do you know this Peter? Are you pair-bonded?"

"What?" she spluttered. "No! Look, what is going on here? All I want is to find Peter and bring him home. If you know where he is, then I demand you take me to him right now!"

"Why? What home does he have to go to? Why would you risk so much to bring him back when he is so alone?"

"W-what do you mean?"

"Who is he to you, Rosemary Watson? If you are not pair-bonded, why are you here? I have to know!"

"I-I—"

He shook her. "Tell me!"

"I love him!" she shouted. "There, are you happy? I've loved him since we first met, but I was just too stupid to figure it out!"

Merius let go of her and Rosemary scrambled away. He stood up and stared over the rumbling water, shaking his head grimly. "Then she has overstepped her bounds."

"'She'? You mean that woman ...," she started. "Her *bounds*? Oh, that's good. That's really good. It's good to know that your bounds stop just short of *kidnapping*!"

Merius gave her a sad smile. "Do not judge us harshly, Rosemary Watson. We thought that Peter was a Lost Child."

"A Lost Child?"

"We once took in dozens of Lost Children. Shipwrecked sailors, too; people who had cut their ties with the world around them and would have drowned if not for us." He sighed. "We gave them a new life. But the sailors stopped coming. The children are all gone, too."

They stood a moment. The wind tugged at Rosemary's clothes and hair. Finally she said, "Whatever. Will you help me bring Peter back?"

He looked at her for another long moment. Then he nodded.

"Thanks," said Rosemary. "How do we do it?"

"I will take you to my people. There, you will challenge the council's claim on Peter."

"A challenge? A simple 'oops, I'm sorry, but we made a mistake' won't suffice?" Her heart fell as he shook his head. "Why not?"

"They will not take my word alone," said Merius. "A powerful woman has taken Peter and I'm something of a ... maverick among my village. The council will need additional convincing."

"Peter will do that. I just have to talk to him."

"Perhaps."

Rosemary jumped to her feet. "Well, let's not just stand here; get me across the lake so I can rescue Peter!"

Merius smiled at her burst of energy. "And how shall I do that, Rosemary Watson?"

"Umm ... boat?"

"I have no boat."

"We walk then. Along the beach?"

He chuckled. "You are at the edge of my world, lass. You could walk straight along this beach forever, and only come in a circle."

She frowned as she tried to put this description together. She gave up quickly. "Well, you got here. Take me the way you came."

"Do you trust me, Rosemary?"

She stepped back and stared at him. "Sure?" she said at last.

"Trust me." He stepped forward and took her hand. Leading her to the water's edge, he waited patiently while Rosemary hesitated. "Trust me."

Rosemary took a deep breath and stepped into the water. She bit her lip at the cold. Merius tugged her forward. She walked until she was knee deep, then waist deep.

When she was chest deep, Merius stopped and gripped her shoulders. "You *do* trust me, Rosemary Watson?"

Rosemary swallowed hard. "I did before you kept asking me! Now, what do we do? Swim?"

"No. Breathe."

He put his hand to her head and pulled her underwater.

Submerged, Rosemary could only look at the murky lake floor. Then she tried to stand up, but Merius pressed her down.

Realization struck her with a blast of bubbles. She tried to push back, to turn her head, get a breath, but Merius wouldn't let her.

She screamed, wasting precious air. She became a flurry of arms, legs, and bubbles as she fought for her life. Her lungs ached, began to beg. She could feel the cold water on her tongue, in her sinuses, at the back of her throat.

"It's not fair!" she cried. Then she gasped. She could yell. She wasn't drowning. She was floundering on her back in water. Wasn't she face-down a moment ago?

She looked around. She was in a shallow bay where the wind did not blow as strong or as cold. Cliffs rose ahead of her and a lake stretched behind her, reminding her of home.

Then she became aware of Merius crouching beside her, a hand on her shoulders, holding her steady. She raised spray scrambling to her feet. "You drowned me!"

Merius smiled darkly. "And yet you live."

She batted his hand away. "No! You tried to drown me!"

Merius laughed. The bass quality of it resonated in her chest. "It was necessary."

"Necessary?!" She clutched her chest. Her lungs were free of water; there wasn't even a tickle in her throat. Except for being wet (again!), she was unharmed. "Why didn't you tell me what you were doing instead of pulling me underwater like that?!"

"Rosemary, if I told you to stick your head underwater and take a deep breath, could you have done so?"

"Maybe, if you had told me!"

Merius just looked at her.

Rosemary looked away. "Okay. No."

He shook his head. "You cannot just walk into our world. You must fall into it, or be pulled through."

"Is that what happened to Peter?"

Merius nodded. "Do you forgive me?"

Rosemary gave him a long look. "What do we do now?"

"I take you to my village."

"Fine. Where is your village?"

Merius pointed to the cliffs. Rosemary shook off his helping hand and splashed towards the shore. She trekked ahead of Merius along the beach. It was only when she reached the gully that she stopped, struck by the familiarity of it all. She stared over the cove, picking out all the landmarks of home.

Merius stepped beside her. "You are not mistaken, Rosemary. This world is a reflection. An echo, a memory."

"Then where was I?"

"The halfway point. When you travel to your reflection, you must first pass through the glass of the mirror itself. A dangerous place."

"Oh." She shook away the strangeness. "Peter."

"Follow me."

They climbed the gully and emerged onto the plateau where Clarksbury would be, had it been there. Rosemary didn't see Merius's village until he abruptly pulled her behind the cover of a tree.

"A simple 'quick, hide' would do, you know!"

"Sorry." Merius pointed. Rosemary looked ahead.

She frowned, trying to figure out what she was seeing. At first, she thought she was looking at another set of cliffs, or possibly a grouping of flowerpot islands — pillars of eroded brown stone with tufts of vegetation on top, of the sort that stuck out into Georgian Bay near her home. Then she saw caves and blob-like windows broken into the columns of stone, and sirens walking in between. She thought of a gigantic sandcastle that had been broken apart by waves. The walkways between the sandy columns wound like the synapses of a mind.

Merius eased her back. "It is important that you not be seen."

Rosemary's eyes narrowed. "I thought I was supposed to challenge their claim on Peter."

"You will. When the time is right."

"I'm not good with patience."

"Then you shall have to practise." He cast a quick glance at the village. "The one who brought Peter here will not take your challenge lightly. We must take her by surprise."

"Mortal combat isn't involved in this challenge, is it?"

"I'm not sure."

Rosemary threw up her hands. "All right, I'll follow your lead ... so long as your plan to smuggle me into the village doesn't involve me tied up in a sack."

Merius blinked at her.

Rosemary gasped in amazed frustration. "That *was* your plan for smuggling me into the village, wasn't it?" Her voice rose until Merius cast nervous glances around for potential eavesdroppers. "No, you find a better way. I've fallen off a cliff, nearly frozen to death, been attacked by salamander-piranhas, squid, and a woman who sealed my face in ice! And you tried to drown me! I am *not* having a good day! I will not cap it off with being tied into a sack and smuggled inside a hostile village. Think of something else!"

***

Merius strode into his village, a heavy sack hoisted over his shoulder.

"I can't believe you talked me into this," the sack muttered.

"If you had thought of a better method, I would have used it," Merius shot back.

"Why does this sack smell of fish?"

"Quiet!"

"Merius!" cried a youthful, joyful voice, tenor to Merius's bass. "Good catch?"

Rosemary's groan cut off abruptly as Merius jounced the sack.

"Yes," he coughed. "The water has been good to me."

"I look forward to the feast," said the man, passing.

"I promise a few surprises," Merius called back. Then he resumed his stride.

"Do you have to bounce so much while you walk?" Rosemary muttered.

"Hush. This is a public street."

"Merius!" a woman called. "Have you heard? Fionarra has returned with a boy!"

"Yes," said Merius. "I was there when she brought him home."

"You were?" Surprise clouded the woman's voice. Then she said, "Ah! I see Eleanna sent you for food for the Homecoming feast. You work fast! Fare thee well!"

"Fare thee well." Merius strode on and Rosemary heard the voices and footfalls withdraw as he turned off the thoroughfare and into a narrower walkway.

"Are we there yet?"

"Hush," said Merius. "Almost. But until I have you in my home, you must remain silent."

Rosemary huffed.

Then she heard a voice, muffled through an open window, that made her freeze.

"... mentioned that yesterday," said Peter. "What is the 'Homecoming'?"

Another voice. "It is a ritual. It is performed when one of our number returns to us. It will reintroduce you to your people — emotionally, socially, and physically."

Then the voices faded as Merius walked on. Rosemary noted the location and kept track of how long Merius walked and whether he walked straight, or turned left or right.

Finally, he entered a silent room, and swung the sack off his shoulder, plunking it on the floor.

"Ow!" Rosemary struggled out of the sack.

"Sorry." Merius closed his door. "You are heavier than the fish I usually carry. That was my fish sack we were using."

"So I guessed." Rosemary sniffed her arms and groaned at the fish smell.

Merius evidently lived inside a shell. The room was a sweeping arch, warm with a sourceless light. There was a mishmash of furniture, too, looking as if it were floating in the pinkness: bookcase, rocking chair, a hurricane lamp on a spindly plant stand. Merius hung the fishy sack on a spiny patch of wall.

"Okay, here I am, all smuggled," said Rosemary. "What do we do now?"

"We wait."

"Wait?!" Rosemary threw up her hands. "You can't be serious!"

"Deadly serious!" Merius snapped. "We cannot confront the council blindly. You shall wait here while I find out exactly what Fionarra has done. Only after that can we plan."

Rosemary stomped her foot, but Merius silenced her with a glare. "Wait here," he repeated, and strode out of sight around a spiral turn of the room. She heard his footsteps, then nothing but the blood in her ears, like the ocean inside a shell. Evidently, there was no door to slam.

"Wait?" she muttered. "Like hell."

CHAPTER NINE
FURY AND PASSION

This time Peter sat in a canoe. A life jacket hugged his shoulders. His parents dipped their paddles into the waters of Georgian Bay.

His mother looked back at him and smiled. Peter beamed at her, then his brow furrowed. He couldn't see her face clearly. Its edges were blurred. He blinked to clear his vision, but the fog grew.

It was all around them. The blue sky turned grey. The horizon vanished.

"Where are we?" said his mother. "Where's the shore?"

"Ahead of us," said his father, his voice firmly reassuring.

"How do you know?"

"It was on our starboard when the fog rolled in," he said. "I turned our boat that way."

"Are you sure?"

"Keep paddling. We'll see the shore soon."

His mother twisted in her seat, worry clear in her voice. "Wait!" She pointed behind them. "Isn't that the lighthouse?"

"Can't be."

"It is! You turned us around!"

Peter turned, struggling against his hugging life jacket. A pinprick of light flashed at them.

The foghorn moaned across the distance, shuddering in Peter's chest.

The vague shape that was his father stared in blank astonishment as the pinprick of light flashed again. "Oh, my God," he breathed.

Then water lapped at Peter's feet. He cried out. "Mommy! We're sinking!"

The foghorn wailed again. The lighthouse flashed once, and then again.

The water in their boat was three inches deep.

"Do something!" his mother shouted.

"We can fix this," his father yelled. He stumbled forward, reaching for a pail. "We got to bale. You need to —"

The boat tipped. Peter screamed and grabbed the sides.

"No!" his mother gasped. "Don't rock the boat! Don't —"

There was a splash. The water was shockingly cold.

The life jacket pulled Peter to the surface where he whacked his head on a paddle. The jacket pinioned his arms and pointed his face to the sky. His legs dangled beneath him. He was too shocked and too small to fight against the buoyancy enough to look around.

He could hear his parents screaming and splashing, calling his name. Eventually, the splashing stopped.

"Mommy?" Silence. "Daddy?"

The fog closed in around him. Lights appeared, on the horizon and beneath his freezing feet, gathering like fireflies.

He slipped beneath the water ...

... and woke with a gasp. "Mom!" He scrambled out of a coffin-like enclosure and landed on the floor with a bump.

"Peter?"

Peter started, then looked up. Ariel stood at his feet, staring at him.

"You screamed," she said.

"Uh," he said, his cheeks flushing. He resisted the urge to hug the life jacket to his chest. "I think I was dreaming. I'm sorry. I'm okay."

He was clinging to the side of a capsized canoe. Or rather, a bed made from a canoe, in tangled waves of blankets. He tried to piece together how he'd gotten in that bed. You ought to remember climbing into a canoe, right? But ... Fiona had kissed him. After that, he just remembered fog.

Ariel was still standing in front of him, biting at her little lip.

"Really, I'm okay," he said, and tried to straighten the coverlets around him.

"You were shouting for our mom."

"I'm sorry." He opened his arms for a hug, and Ariel climbed on him and gave his neck a squeeze. There was a lumpy something wedged between them. "What's this?" he asked, trying to comfort her. "Am I squishing breakfast in bed?"

Ariel shook her head and held up a bundle of cloth. "I brought you your Homecoming robes."

Peter unrolled a bolt of cloth. He could stare through it: it was transparent as a veil of water. "It's sort of ...," he started, and for some reason he remembered Fiona kissing him and blushed furiously.

Ariel giggled. "You wear it over your own clothes, silly!" Ariel went over to the steamer trunk and opened it, revealing bolts of green cloth and leather belts. She pulled out a green tunic.

Peter held the tunic out. "What about my pants?"

Ariel stared at him.

He shrugged and slipped the tunic over his t-shirt. "Thanks." He shifted uneasily on his feet, but Ariel didn't leave.

"Aren't you going to put the robes on?" she asked.

"What, now?"

"Eleanna wants to be sure they fit. The ceremony's today."

"Well, I ...." Peter went over to the freckled mirror and wrapped the cloth around himself. He frowned irritably when Ariel laughed. "What's wrong?"

"Not that way!" she said. "Here, let me."

Peter sighed and tried to stand like a mannequin as Ariel tied one end of the bolt around his belt and began wrapping it around his body, twisting once for every turn.

As the cloth draped over him, he couldn't help but chuckle. Rosemary would split her sides if she saw him.

He stopped. Rosemary.

There was a knock at his door. Peter jumped. Before he could say anything, the knob turned and Fiona entered, bearing a tray of fishcakes and sliced fruit.

Ariel gave him a quick squeeze. "I'll come back." She darted around Fiona and bolted down the hall. Fiona smiled to see Peter's robes. "You look wonderful!"

He chuckled. "If you say so. Is this breakfast?"

"Yes." She set the tray on a table by the window and proffered a mug. "We brewed you some coffee."

Peter pulled off the swaths of cloth, still feeling self-conscious in his tunic. He took the mug and sniffed it. "By the way you say that, you're not normally coffee drinkers, are you?"

"We are becoming so," said Fiona.

Peter gulped the coffee gratefully. Then he saw Fiona standing, doing nothing but waiting. He cleared his throat. "Would you like to join me?" He indicated the table with its tray.

Fiona's smile widened. She sat down, taking her own plate from the tray. The two ate in silence with their fingers, Peter casting glances at Fiona and trying, but failing, to find something to say.

At last, when they had cleaned their plates, Fiona gave him a patient smile. "You have more questions. Say them, Peter."

Peter hesitated. "About last night" was not the way he wanted to start his next sentence. After some thought, he said, "I can't remember what happened last night after you ...," he coughed, "... kissed me."

Fiona blinked at him. "You got tired and fell asleep. I tucked you into bed. Should anything else have happened?"

Peter flushed pink. Fiona laughed lightly. "You know how I feel about you, Peter. However, there are many rituals and ceremonies we would have to go through before anything else would be allowed to happen. Even before that, you must pass through the Homecoming."

"Yes, somebody mentioned that yesterday," said Peter. "What is the 'Homecoming'?"

"It is a ritual. It is performed when one of our number returns to us. It will reintroduce you to your people — emotionally, socially, and physically."

"Physically?"

"You will become like us."

"Aren't I already like you?"

"I told you that you were not human, Peter. But you have lived with them for most of your life. You were changed for this. That's why they call such children 'changelings.'"

"I thought they were called 'changelings' because the baby was changed with the duplicate."

"That is the human definition," said Fiona quickly. "My point is, you may not notice the differences between us at first, but they are there. Perhaps you notice how your mind is so often fogged. At the ceremony, this will end. We will change you back."

"That won't be too difficult, will it? You don't have to cut things off, or rearrange organs, or anything like that?"

"I promise you, the ceremony is quite painless."

There was another knock on the door and Ariel entered. She stepped up to Fiona and beckoned her down. "Your mother calls for you. There is news you should attend to." A look passed between them, and Fiona stood up.

"Excuse me, Peter," she said.

"Anything serious?"

"No. Enjoy your coffee." She followed Ariel from the room. Peter watched her go until the door cut off his vision like wood blocking a magnet.

He sat blinking for a moment, rubbing his forehead. Then, taking his coffee, he slid his chair back. He stepped to the window and peered through the glass.

He found himself staring across the village park. He saw the stone amphitheatre and the thin houses on the other side. The cliff face shimmered in the distance, and as Peter watched, the shimmering grew. The lines of the houses blurred. Peter winced and clutched his eyes. He turned from the window.

"Peter!"

Peter perked up. He wasn't dreaming. He looked around the room, and his stare settled upon a face peering in through the window. He hadn't heard it open.

"Peter!" Rosemary hissed. Her hair fluttered in the breeze. "Pete— whoop!" Something gave way beneath her and she vanished from the frame. Her fingers whitened on the sill and she hauled herself back into view. "Peter!"

Peter set down his mug and ran over. "Rosemary, what are you doing there?"

"Wishing I was taller! Give me a hand!"

Peter grabbed Rosemary's arms and pulled. When Rosemary was almost through, she snagged her foot on the sill and tumbled, knocking them both into a sprawling heap on the bedroom floor.

Peter jumped up and helped her to her feet. Taking a second to see that it was really her, he embraced her, pressing his face into her hair.

"Peter?" Rosemary's voice was muffled by his tunic. "What on Earth are you wearing?"

He pushed her back, holding her by the shoulders, staring at her in disbelief. "How did you get here?"

"Same as you!" She frowned at his blank expression. "Don't you remember falling off the cliff?"

Her scream echoed in his head. How could he have forgotten? "My God, Rosemary, are you okay?"

"Never mind that!" She took his hand. "We're getting out of here."

His heart leapt as he approached the window. He stared at it as if it were a cliff he had to climb. "No."

"Come on, Peter!" She tugged him. "We've got to go home!"

"No!"

Rosemary's gaze hit him like a punch in the stomach, but he didn't falter. "I can't. I won't. I belong here."

"What?" There was a dangerous edge to Rosemary's voice. Her eyes were wide with rejection and anger. "What do you mean, you belong here?"

"These are my people. They came to take me back."

"Your people? What are you talking about? These people kidnap you, and you want to stay?"

"It's not like that —"

"And what about me?" she cut in. "After all I went through finding you —"

"I didn't ask you to follow me!"

"Damn it, Peter, I deserve an explanation, at least!" She jerked up her bandaged arm. "I went through a swarm of piranhas to find you! I almost froze to death!"

Peter stared at her bandage, its spot of blood the size of a quarter.

"You're hurt!" he yelled, grabbing her wrist, letting it go when she gasped with pain. "W-what happened?"

Rosemary stared at him. "Peter?"

He stumbled. His knees wobbled. His mind was whirling, screaming at itself.

Rosemary has come to take me home.

This is home. There's nothing for you in Clarksbury.

But there was Rosemary, and here she is. She's come to take me home!

His knees buckled.

Then he heard footsteps in the hall, and the effect disappeared. "Peter?" Fiona's voice.

He looked around frantically. "Quick! Hide!"

Rosemary stared at him. She didn't move. "What are you talking about?"

"They can't find you here!" Fear for Rosemary clutched his throat, though he couldn't figure out why. "Hide in the closet! In the closet!" He grabbed her by the waist and hauled her across the room.

"Let go of me!" Rosemary punched him so hard he was still retching when the door burst open.

Fiona stood in the doorway, trident in her hand, her mother and Ariel behind her. She took in the sight of Peter on his knees, and Rosemary standing, fists raised, in the middle of the room. She focussed on Rosemary, and her gaze grew dark. "You!"

"She's my friend, Fiona," Peter gasped.

Fiona hoisted her trident at Rosemary. The shaft gleamed. "I'm warning you, don't interfere!"

"Fiona!" Peter wheezed.

"Some welcoming party, Peter," said Rosemary, backing away.

"Fiona, what are you doing?" Peter scrambled to his feet and grabbed Fiona's trident. There was a sizzling sound and he cried out. The shaft left a red mark across both palms.

"Peter!" both women cried. Fiona dropped her trident and rushed for the shocked boy, arriving a split second after Rosemary. She pushed Rosemary aside, but Rosemary resisted.

Peter looked up from his hands, and shook his head blearily. Fiona wavered in front of him. Her skin flickered green and he saw the ghost of fins on her arms. "What?" he mumbled, as though waking from a dream. "Who ... Ariel?"

Fiona's image solidified. Rosemary pulled hard at Fiona's hair. Fiona had her hand around Rosemary's throat.

"Stop fighting," he gasped. Then he shouldered between them. "Fiona, stop it!" he yelled. "Rosemary is my friend; stop fighting!"

Both women glared at each other. Then Fiona relented. "I am sorry, Peter. I was taken by surprise. Do your hands hurt?" She reached for him ... but for his eyes, not his hands.

"Hey!" Rosemary shouted.

Fiona touched Peter's brow. He fell to his knees.

Dimly, he could hear Rosemary screaming. "What did you do to him?"

"Take her away! We can decide what to do with her next council meeting!" Did Fiona say this?

More people were rushing into his room.

"Intruder!" Eleanna shouted. "She attacked Peter!"

"No, I didn't!" Rosemary yelled.

Fiona lowered him to the bed. Yes, sleep seemed just the thing for him, now.

"Peter!" Rosemary cried. "Peter!"

He felt that he should care. He felt it strange that he could not.

"Peter!"

He slipped into a deep sleep, and Fiona dominated his dreams.

CHAPTER TEN
SWEET AIR

Peter struggled awake and rolled out of his canoe-bed. "I mustn't sleep," he gasped. "Mustn't sleep!"

He sat up, rubbing his eyes in confusion. Why mustn't he sleep?

All at once, the answer came to him.

"Rosemary!"

He scrambled up and looked around the room. He was alone. Bringing his breathing under control, he stepped to the door and opened it a crack. He heard voices outside.

"That woman!" Fiona stormed. "She'll ruin everything! I could have ripped her to shreds where she stood!"

"That was her," said another voice, soft and lilting, but full of fear. "Darius and I saw her on the edge of our world. She is a songbreaker, Fionarra! She robbed me of my second with just one word from her lips."

Fiona hissed. "A songbreaker! And to think I just left her out there. But she could not have got in here without help. Someone must have pulled her in, Loria."

"Merius?" said Loria.

"Merius. He'd do anything to embarrass me before the council. He might even be stupid enough to bring a songbreaker amongst us. Wait till Eleanna hears this. Yes, she *will* hear of this."

"But what about the songbreaker?"

"Does anybody else know what she is?" asked Fiona.

"No, only Darius and I saw her powers."

"Then do not talk about her to anyone else."

"But —"

"We must not cause a panic. At least not until I can be sure that Merius is behind this. Then I will expose his treachery."

"Is your rivalry with Merius all you can think of? We have a songbreaker in the village! We have to make her leave. If she is linked with Peter, then perhaps —"

"No."

"But —"

"No! I will *not* send Peter away after all that I've risked. Peter belongs here!"

Peter shut the door quickly but quietly. He had to think, and to do that, he didn't want to hear Fiona's voice, even in the next room.

He leaned against the wall. So, Rosemary had followed him to this world, or had fallen into it. Judging from Fiona's tone of voice, she wasn't welcome here.

How could a people who had accepted him reject somebody like Rosemary?

The dominant voice in his head spoke out: Because she's human and you're not. You belong here and she does not.

And yet he knew Rosemary well enough to know that she would not leave without him.

The battle of wills between Rosemary and Fiona played out in his mind, with this "council" standing behind Fiona. He knew he had to make Rosemary leave, for her own sake. To do that, he had to talk to her. And he sensed the council and Fiona would frown upon that.

So, the council and Fiona had better not see him talk to Rosemary.

Stepping to the window, he pushed up the casement and hauled himself over the sill.

Behind him, the door clicked. Ariel sidled in and stared at the empty room. Her eyes fell upon the window.

***

Rosemary paced her bar-less cage. She followed the perimeter of a bubble-shaped cave, tapping her fingers on the rough stone wall. Small nooks and crannies glowed phosphor, providing the only light. There was no window. There was no door. There was no hole in the ceiling, and yet somehow they'd thrown her in here.

No, there had to be some sense to this. Every cell had an exit, or else they couldn't have gotten her in here, so she circled the blob-shaped room, treading carefully on the uneven floor, feeling for any difference in the texture of the wall.

On her third circuit, she found something.

She stopped and ran her fingers along the rough stone. It felt as hard as granite, and then she passed a spot where the stone pushed back, but without any sense of touch, like an air mattress, but without the mattress.

Rosemary pushed harder. She saw her fingers whiten; her tips felt numb, but as she pressed, she saw the fingers begin to vanish into the stone. She ran her other along the wall and felt the same thing. The space between her two hands was wide enough for a door.

"A-ha!" she muttered. She flattened her hands on the smooth surface, and saw her fingers sink beneath the stone. "I knew it!" Just like these creatures to try to fool her into staying in her cell.

She pushed at the space. She put her shoulder in it. She put her back on it and scuffed her feet. Each time she bounced back like she was fighting elastic. In the end, she slumped to the floor, breathing heavily.

Then the wall opposite her shimmered, and a cave entrance materialized. Merius stepped through, bearing his trident. The opening vanished once he was in the centre of the room.

"Is any of this place real?" she asked.

"It's all as real as we want it to be," said Merius. He nodded over his shoulder the way he'd come. "Did they hurt you?"

"No." Rosemary stood up. "And I admit I gave them plenty of reasons to."

Merius smirked. "Good."

"Really?"

"Only in its context," said Merius. "I appreciate that you stand up for yourself, but you were still a fool to confront Fionarra when I wasn't ready."

Rosemary frowned at him. "I heard Peter's voice when you smuggled me into your home. I thought that if I could talk to him —"

"You'd find yourself in a room with no doors?"

Rosemary glared. "I *had* to try. I almost reached him, too, until this woman burst in and touched his eyes."

"Ah," said Merius, nodding. "That was Fionarra. I *thought* she was using glamour to keep Peter under her thumb."

"Glamour?"

"It is the singing of our minds made solid," said Merius. "Applied by voice or touch, it allows us to control what people see, even ourselves. From this we create our tools, our nets, our homes ..."

"Doors that look like walls?" Rosemary asked. "Even other people?" A small army to hunt down large creatures like squid, she thought.

Merius nodded. "Glamour is at the foundation of our society."

"And that's what's holding Peter? How do I fight it?"

"You don't," Merius rumbled. "You can break glamour for a few seconds, through some shock like cold water, a kiss, or a firebrand, but unless blocked by an exceptionally strong mind, glamour simply reasserts itself."

Rosemary started to say something, but Merius cut her off. "Don't raise your hopes high. Peter is a man, and the human male is notoriously susceptible to glamour. Moreover, there is a second glamour behind the first. Fionarra could not have called him to this world unless, deep down, Peter wanted to come. Even if you could break Peter's external glamour, you would not have time to break through his internal glamour, his desire to find a family here, before the external glamour reasserted itself."

"I have to try," snapped Rosemary.

"Rosemary!"

"Peter!" She whirled around and found herself staring at a small, blob-shaped window on the wall over her shoulder. Peter stood on the other side, gripping the sill. She ran up to him.

"Keep out of sight," said Peter, looking nervously over his shoulder. "Nobody can see me talking to you."

She looked past him, into a gully cut between two rises of rock. "Peter, what —" She looked at his feet and started. "How the heck did you get up here?"

He frowned at her. "What? I'm just standing on a box."

Rosemary craned her neck. He stood on an outcrop, his heels in midair, fifteen feet above uneven ground.

"Peter," said Merius.

Peter gasped and stumbled back. Horrified, Rosemary grabbed him through the window and pulled him back to the sill. "It's okay," she said before he could run. "This is Merius. He's a ...." She looked Merius up and down. "He's an ally. You can talk in front of him."

"Peter," said Merius again. "Does Fionarra know you're here?"

"No," said Peter. "And she'd better not find out, so listen up, Rosemary: you've got to leave!"

She bristled. "Not without you!"

"I'll make sure Fiona gets you back to Clarksbury, but I'm staying here."

"Peter!" She gripped his hand. "Listen to me! They're lying to you! You're *not* one of them; you're not even green!"

Merius blinked. "Green?"

"Peter, please," she continued. "You've got to come home with me!"

Peter glared at her. "Why? My parents are dead, my uncle's never home! I have no friends; I'm treated like a stranger. These sirens, I may not be like them now, but the Homecoming Ceremony will take care of that. There's nothing left for me in Clarksbury."

Rosemary's eyes glistened and she swallowed hard. "But ... what about me?"

There was a long pause. Peter couldn't look her in the eye. "Rosemary ... j-just leave me and go ... I'm ... I'm back where I belong." He pulled free from her grip and hopped off the outcrop, landing lightly on the ground.

"Peter, come back!" Rosemary reached through the window, and strained against its sides. "Peter!" She struggled as Merius plucked her free.

"Careful!" he gasped. "Peter is right: he mustn't be seen near you."

Rosemary slumped against the wall, choking back tears. "He wouldn't listen to me," she sobbed. "He's too tied up in their lies!"

Merius patted her shoulder. "Actually, I was impressed by him."

She looked up. "What do you mean?"

"If Peter were truly under Fionarra's grip, would he have cared enough to sneak away and tell you to leave?"

She brightened. "You mean I have a chance?"

"I think Fionarra doesn't have the hold over Peter that she thinks she has. Are you sure you two aren't pair-bonded?"

Rosemary blushed. "Certain." She drew herself up. "Let's get out of here and figure out how to reach him."

"I have a plan already," said Merius. "You stay here."

Rosemary frowned. "Stuck in this cell?"

"Here, Fionarra would think you were safely tucked away. It would lower her guard."

"Of course, because I'd *be* under guard. At least release me into your custody, or something!"

Merius shook his head. "Officially, I am here to question you and determine if the council's decision to return you to your world is the correct one. I will leave, and state that I agree with the council's decision. With the council's suspicions off me, I can plan how to confront Fionarra."

"That's not a plan at all!"

"I will not jeopardize my position on council. Right now, Fionarra faces uncomfortable questions over how you came to be here. If it comes out that *I* helped to bring you here, then it will be *my* position that is threatened!"

Rosemary spluttered. "Did you save my life just to make me your political pawn?"

"You misunderstand," said Merius. "Fionarra violated protocol. For that, I shall make sure she faces the consequences."

"You don't care about me or Peter at all! I was right the first time: there *is* nothing good in this world!"

"Do not test my patience, Rosemary Watson!" And with a roar, Merius transformed into a huge, smoking dragon that towered over her. His wings touched the sides of the cell; his breath singed Rosemary's cheeks.

She stumbled back. "Stop it!"

The dragon vanished, leaving Merius, arms raised, caught in mid jump. He scrambled back, fumbling like a man in a crowd who had suddenly found himself naked. "What did you do?"

"What did *I* do? What did *you* just do?"

"I changed myself to make you appreciate my authority," said Merius. "But I couldn't keep up the song. How do I look to you now? Describe me!"

"You look the same as when I first saw you," Rosemary huffed. When he prodded her, she added, "You're tall, you've got green skin, and you have fins on the back of your arms and legs. You're just like everybody in this crazy place."

Merius leaned back, horrified. The wall stopped his fall. "You saw me thus from the beginning? I did not look like one of your kind?"

"Not even close!"

"You can see through me," Merius breathed. "You can break my song. The mark on your hand must be the mark of a songbreaker!"

"That's what the other two sirens said," said Rosemary. She drew herself up, "So, what does this have to do about anything?" She stepped forward menacingly. "Tell me now or I'll break more of your songs! You know I can!"

"Yes, you can." Fear faded from his eyes, replaced with resignation. "Indeed, you could disassemble the very bonds that hold this civilization together."

Rosemary stopped. "W-what?" She started to back away.

Merius picked up his trident. "You cannot stay here, and the council must never find out that I brought you here or my life would be forfeit. You are too dangerous to let live."

He lunged. Rosemary scrambled away just before his trident cracked the wall behind her.

She ran for the cell door, screaming for help, and stopped when she found only smooth wall. No help came. Instinct made her duck and the trident sailed over her head. She rolled up and tried to wrench the weapon from his grip, but Merius held on and threw her against the wall.

She fought back, kicking and punching. One of her kicks landed solidly between his legs, but he barely flinched. She clawed at his eyes, but her arms weren't long enough.

He thrust her back against the wall and pressed the cold shaft of the trident to her throat. She could feel the granite bruising her shoulder blades.

"Merius!" she gasped. Tears ran down her cheeks. "Please! I just want to bring Peter home!"

"I'm sorry," he said, stone-faced. He pressed down on the shaft, and Rosemary could only gurgle. Her feet kicked uselessly. Darkness crept into the edge of her vision.

Then the wall behind her gave way like the icy crust of a snowdrift. She was a split-second in darkness, and then falling through open air, landing heavily on the ground.

Through her whirling senses, the burning of her throat, and the screaming relief of her lungs, she barely registered the sound of shocked voices. She was at the bottom of a gap between two stone pillars, near where the gully opened out onto a clearing. A dozen people stared at her, their voices rising in fear.

"She came through the wall!"

"She came through the song!"

"Glamour can't bind her!"

"She's a songbreaker!"

Above her, Rosemary saw only a stone wall, with no hole that she could have fallen through. Merius glared at her through the window.

She staggered up, clutching her throat, but was too disoriented to run. People were shouldering through the crowd, homing in on her, bearing tridents.

"This way," said a little girl's voice. "Run this way!"

Rosemary could see nobody around her, but instinct made her follow the voice deeper into the gully.

The crowd charged.

Rosemary stumbled. Her vision swam. Her throat ached to breathe, much less swallow.

"You must hurry!" said the little girl's voice. "They're almost upon us!"

The gap between the stones narrowed, branched, and twisted. Rosemary missed a turn and careened into a wall, but the voice urged her on. The sounds of their pursuers faded.

Then Rosemary stumbled into a dead-end. The cliff stretched up, impossible to climb. She gasped in horror.

"It's okay," the voice breathed. "Rest. I'll hide you."

A shadow cloaked the entrance to the branch.

Rosemary collapsed against the base of the cliff.

The sound of running feet came closer, and halted at the junction.

"Where is she?"

"She can't have disappeared."

"That way leads out of the village. She has found her way back into the wilderness!"

"We have to organize a search party. Get Fionarra!"

The voices dispersed. Alone, Rosemary slumped over and fell unconscious.

There was a moment's silence, then Ariel stepped out of her own shadow. Looking down all the branches of the junction, she made sure that they were alone. In the distance, the mob clamoured to be organized.

She turned back to Rosemary and put a hand on her forehead. "For your safety, sleep until the village is quiet."

Rosemary shifted, and began to breathe more easily.

After checking that Rosemary was safely hidden, Ariel crept back the way she'd come, heading towards home.

CHAPTER ELEVEN
NOTHING THAT FADES

Peter slipped through the village, following the shadows to Fiona's home. He walked so carefully, wary of being seen, it took him a while to realize that the village was quiet. He stopped, listening, and then stepped out to the middle of an intersection of two alleyways. In every direction he looked, there was no one around to see him.

"What the ..."

He finally heard voices as he approached the central park. He ducked behind cover as nine villagers trooped past, hoisting tridents.

He waited until they turned a corner, and then slipped out. The village was silent again. He walked boldly through the back alleyways, keeping an ear open, but not keeping to the shadows, until he found his bedroom window. He hauled himself through.

The bedroom was as he'd left it. He nodded to himself, satisfied: no one knew he had snuck out.

Why should I have had to sneak out like that? he thought. Aren't I welcome here? And why should I be so afraid for Rosemary if these people are as welcoming as I think them to be?

The fog curled in his mind, as though at the beginning of a clear, crisp wind.

So much didn't make sense. I belong here, don't I? What could still be eating at my heart?

He needed answers. And in a flash, he knew who could give them to him.

Peter stepped out into the hall, past the quiet rooms. He stopped short when he heard a knock on the front door. He ducked into the bathroom and held the door open a crack, listening.

Fiona breezed past, her beauty as bright as blood. The door swung open. "What is it?"

"The songbreaker has escaped," said Loria. "She slipped through the wall of her cell. Merius was with her. We are organizing a search party."

"Merius was with her?" Grim satisfaction edged her voice. "Good. Gather the search party at the edge of the village. And wait for us. Before we go, I'm summoning Merius. I'm sure Eleanna will be interested in what he has to say."

She swept to the kitchen. Peering out, Peter saw her

emerge and step out the front door. The door slammed behind her.

Peter was about to leave the bathroom when movement sent him skittering back. Eleanna shuffled out of the kitchen and slipped into the front room. He waited for silence, and then crept down the hallway, focusing on the playroom behind the front room. He stepped inside. To his surprise, it was empty.

The front door opened and closed softly. Ariel stood in the entranceway, her young face in a pensive frown. She stepped to her playroom, stopping short in astonishment. "Peter —"

He put his fingers to his lips.

"What is it?" she whispered.

"Can we speak outside?"

Ariel followed, staring but not questioning as Peter snuck past the living room and out the front door. They stood a moment in the front yard. The central park was empty. The other houses were silent. Finally, Peter spoke.

"Ariel," said Peter. "Is Rosemary all right?"

Ariel hesitated. Then she nodded.

"Why is Fiona searching for her?"

Ariel swallowed, but she looked Peter in the eye. "The council believes that she has escaped into the wilderness."

"What will they do if they find her?"

Ariel gave Peter a firm, earnest look. "They will not harm her." Then she bit her lip and looked away. Her hands clenched and unclenched. Suddenly, she wrapped her arms around him and began to sob. "Peter, I want you to stay and be my brother. I'm so lonely here!"

"Hey, it's okay." He crouched down and hugged her. "I'm not going anywhere. Don't cry."

She sobbed into his shoulder a moment longer. Then she pushed herself away. "I'm sorry," she sniffed.

He sat on the ground and laughed sadly. "Look at us. We're going to be lonely wherever we live."

Ariel looked at him. "But now we're together."

"We're just two people, Ariel. Two people can be as lonely as one. But at least we can be lonely together, wherever we are."

"But we belong here," said Ariel.

"You do." He sighed. "I'm not sure about me. I spent over half my life with parents I didn't realize were adopted, and the rest of my life as an orphan." He drew himself up. "Ariel, I need to know where my parents — our birth parents — are buried."

Ariel's brow furrowed. "Buried?"

"Yes. Where's your graveyard?"

"Graveyard?"

Peter frowned. "Where do you put your dead?"

She gasped. "You wish to visit the burning grounds? Nobody goes there!"

Peter spluttered. "How do you remember your dead?"

Ariel stopped. Finally, she said, "What do you need, Peter?"

He took a deep breath. "I need to know that I'm a part of this place. I need to find some place where our parents are, where I can remember them."

The light came on behind Ariel's eyes. She took his hand. "Follow me."

She led him across the central park, past a wooden stage being raised on the stone amphitheatre that reminded him of a dry wading pool. Peter hadn't noticed anybody working on this before, but Ariel tugged him forward before he could think about what it meant. She took him on the path to the bay.

As they stumbled down the steep and rocky slope, he could hear the breakers below. They rounded a corner of the escarpment, and the lake stretched before them. The warm, moist wind touched his cheeks and ruffled his hair. And still Ariel walked, tugging his hand whenever he hesitated. They were on the beach, heading for the large boulder where he'd first seen Ariel. It stood, shorn from the cliffs, just short of the water's edge. A scraggly tree grew on top.

Ariel stopped before the great rock. She pointed at the tree, then out towards the lake. Peter looked at her, befuddled.

"There," she said, pointing at the top of the rock again. "Sit there. That is where I go to remember the dead."

★ ★ ★

In her hideaway, Rosemary eased awake. She tried to swallow and wondered why it hurt, so. Then she remembered and she sat up with a start, clutching her throat.

She took a deep, calming breath, swallowed, grimaced, and pieced together the chase and her surroundings. She was not dead. She was not in a cell. The gaps between the stone pillars were quiet. The wind whistled through the gullies. She was safe, for now.

She stood up and crept back to the junction. It was silent there too, even in the surrounding houses.

"Have they *all* gone looking for me?" she rasped. Even at a whisper, her voice was too loud for the silence.

It could be a trap, but Rosemary doubted it. The silence was not one of secrecy but of emptiness, as though she was in the middle of an evacuated city. It was a gift, unless Peter had been evacuated too. She wouldn't know until she found him.

She looked around, picked the wider branch that angled downhill, and set off in search of Peter's house.

As she walked, she thought about her miraculous escape. Merius had had her up against a wall, strangling her — her heart skipped a beat and she touched her throat — and suddenly the wall had given way ... only it hadn't. She saw that it hadn't.

She remembered Peter standing on a ledge so small, his heels were in midair. He'd said he'd been standing on a box, and had jumped down fifteen feet as if it were nothing. It was clear what Peter was seeing wasn't real. But what she was seeing — what Merius was seeing — might not be real either.

"'You could disassemble the very bonds that hold this civilization together,'" she muttered. "No wonder he was afraid of me." But if what *he* saw wasn't real either, what was?

A picture of the world, glamour wrapped over glamour, whirled before her eyes and she suddenly felt dizzy.

The walls of her prison had held her inside, though, despite her best efforts to push through. Only when Merius was strangling her did the glamour give way. She hadn't thought about making those sirens on the beach disappear, it had just happened. If she was a song-breaker, maybe she was only able to break songs when she wasn't thinking.

She went up to a wall and pressed her hands on the stone. It felt as hard and rough as granite. Then she closed her eyes, thought about nothing, and pushed harder. She felt her wrists sinking, as though through sand. Opening her eyes, she saw her hands embedded in the wall. She pulled out her hands and wiggled her fingers. The wall she left behind was smooth. "Huh!"

She wondered what the place really looked like. Perhaps it was a ruin. Or perhaps it wasn't there at all.

"That trident was real enough," she muttered, shuddering. "I may be able to walk through walls, but they can still bash my head in." She resumed her search.

Eventually, she found the gully near where she'd found Peter and confronted Fiona. She walked cautiously, ears open for any sound, but this gorge echoed with emptiness like all the rest. She found Peter's bedroom window. She was about to haul herself over the sill when she stopped.

"I can walk through walls, remember?" she said. She backed up, scuffed her feet on the ground, and charged.

As she picked herself up and checked her nose for blood, she said, "Okay, so *some* of the walls are real. Noted."

She hauled herself through the window.

She looked around Peter's room, moist like the inside of a cave, and lit by a phosphor glow. Her eyes lingered on the bed, built out of a canoe. She fingered the hand-stitched quilt. She didn't know much about quilts, but she knew a work of art when she saw one.

Then she remembered the woman and her second on that beach with the squid, peering at the shipwrecked furniture. "You're scavengers," she muttered, "taking the things you need from the shipwrecks. Did you sink those ships? I wouldn't put it past you."

She crept to a wooden door that had been cut to fit an opening in the cave wall. Opening it an inch, she listened to the hallway beyond. The place was either empty or asleep. Rosemary staked her life on empty.

She crossed the hallway and tested the first door she came to. It opened onto another cave with sea-green robes scattered around a full-length gilded mirror. A pile of papers lay on a rich, wooden desk that had had its legs cut to level it on the uneven floor. Mismatched utensils and a plate holding crumbs and a dried, half-eaten fishcake lay abandoned.

"Fionarra's room, I bet," Rosemary muttered. She spotted an ornate bookcase wedged between floor and ceiling, laden with leather-bound tomes, and she crept in to investigate. Many of the books were old enough to make collectors weep, and stacked in no order. Bibles and ships' logs rubbed shoulders with the works of Robert Louis Stevenson and Charles Dickens. On a lower shelf were newer, more primitive books; sheets of paper bound by thick thread. Rosemary pulled one out and saw pages of hand-drawn pictures and handwriting, in a language

Rosemary could not read. She closed the book and shelved it, and turned to the desk.

On it, there were maps and nautical charts showing Georgian Bay, decades old but on crisp, white paper. Underneath the maps was another primitive book, opened to a picture. Rosemary couldn't recognize the writing here either, but the picture was drawing of a siren wearing a crown of twelve smaller sirens, and each of these had a crown of their own. Rosemary remembered the two sirens chanting on the stony beach, pulling back, and leaving two more sirens between them.

Was this an instruction manual? If so, why would Fionarra need to read it before she came to Clarksbury to steal Peter?

Beneath that book was another open to a diagram of siren women walking in a solemn circle around two sirens joining hands.

Rosemary put the books down and moved the papers back on top of them. She crept back into the hallway.

Fionarra's bedroom was the only bedroom in the house, other than Peter's. The bathroom revealed a stone tub with no internal plumbing and dried, sweet-smelling seaweed in thick glass bottles. In the kitchen, Rosemary helped herself to a fishcake.

Looking in on a playroom of battered toys, Rosemary stopped. There was only one room left to explore: the front room. She'd found only two bed-rooms in this house: Peter and Fionarra's. Fionarra's bedroom belonged to a teenager. These toys belonged to someone much younger. Where did this child sleep?

Then Rosemary heard her first noise.

She held her breath. The sound beat, *creak-click, creak-click*, as regular as clockwork. Peering into the front room, Rosemary saw a grandfather clock, and laughed at her own fright. She entered, heading for a promising looking bookcase.

As she peered at these books, the clockwork tick continued, *creak-click, creak-click, "Znnnk! Guh!"*

Rosemary carefully set the book she was holding back onto the bookcase and straightened up. Slowly she turned, and looked at the clock.

Its pendulum was dead in its case.

Her heart filled with lead.

Casting her eyes around the room, she spotted movement in a shadowed corner. An old siren woman sat in a rocking chair, *creak-click, creak-click*.

Rosemary stopped breathing until she realized that the woman's eyes were closed. Her soft breath was regular. She was asleep as she rocked.

Okay, she thought. Right. I'm okay. Thank God. I'll just tiptoe out of this room —

The front door burst open with a volley of two voices.

JAMES BOW

"You have no right to threaten me! It was your mistake that sent the songbreaker after us in the first place!" yelled Merius.

"It was your incompetence that led the songbreaker here!" shouted Fionarra.

Rosemary dove beneath a maple dining-room table pressed against the wall. She pushed herself as deep as she could into the shadows.

Merius stormed in, Fionarra hot on his heels. The old woman stopped rocking and looked glassily up as the pair rounded on each other and almost touched noses.

"You compound your offence by blackmailing me!" Merius ranted.

"You sought to embarrass me before the council, except that your plan backfired!"

"How was I to know?"

"A-ha! So you admit it!"

The old woman cleared her throat. "What is going on?"

"I have done nothing to be ashamed of!" shouted Merius. "You are the one who violated the principles of the Homecoming!"

The glassy dullness vanished from the old woman's stare. Her knuckles whitened on the armrests and she stood up. "What is it?" she intoned. Merius and Fionarra fell silent.

"Well?" the old woman continued. "Fionarra, you speak first."

Merius turned aside in disgust as Fionarra drew herself up. "Eleanna, I must report that the girl discovered earlier today in Peter's bedroom is, as the rumours reported, a songbreaker. I have evidence proving that she was led here —" she jabbed a finger at Merius, "— by none other than this incompetent fool!"

Merius rounded on her. "You seek only to cover up your mistake by pointing out another —"

"Leading a songbreaker to this village is a very serious mistake, Merius," said Eleanna firmly. "I wouldn't brush it off lightly. But go on; your point?"

Merius huffed. "My point is, this songbreaker was drawn here. However she passed through the edge of our world, she would not have been looking for us if she had not been tied to our initiate, Peter, and Fionarra knew this!"

Eleanna turned her gaze on Fionarra, who could only stare at the floor. "I asked you before, Fionarra, did you choose well? With this development, I ask again: did you?"

"Yes."

"Are you sure?"

"Yes," Fionarra snapped. "I chose with my heart."

Merius let out a hollow laugh.

"Whatever the dispute between you two," said Eleanna. "Put it aside. There is a songbreaker amongst us. What measures have you taken to protect this village?"

"A search party has been organized," said Fionarra. "I'm leading it."

"Then I'm going too," said Merius at once.

"You —"

"Go! Both of you!" Eleanna snapped. "Your disgraceful rivalry has almost brought ruin to us. Therefore you will *both* search for the songbreaker, and decide how best to nullify her."

Rosemary put a hand to her throat.

Merius and Fionarra glared at each other a moment longer, and then stormed out in silence. Eleanna watched them go, then sagged like a deflated balloon. She touched her back, grimaced, and hobbled across the living room. She leaned against the table under which Rosemary was hiding.

"You can come out, now," she said.

Rosemary banged her head against the tabletop.

CHAPTER TWELVE
TRICKS OF DESPERATION

Peter scrabbled for a foothold, knocking free bits of rock as he hauled himself the rest of the way up the boulder. He turned to lend a hand to Ariel, but she was already crouching beside him.

There was room for the both of them, as well as the tree that gripped tenaciously at the dry stone. They could see far out to the horizon. The waves rumbled in around them and died.

Peter looked to Ariel for guidance. She crawled over the flat part of the stone and sat, cross-legged, looking out at the lake. Peter slid up beside her and did the same.

"What now?" he asked after a while.

"Just remember," she replied. He saw that her eyes were closed, so he closed his own. He took in a deep breath and felt himself relax. He felt as though he was floating above the water, soothed by the hush of the waves.

For a while, he remembered nothing. He just felt his spine relax and the tension ease out of his head. I should do this more often, he thought, before he shushed himself.

"Peter?" Ariel's voice eased across his consciousness.

"Hmm?"

"This Rosemary ... who is she?"

"A friend," he said.

"From your old world?"

He nodded.

"But I thought you had no friends."

"I *did* have friends. Not close friends, but ... and I had her. She was my best friend."

"How did you two meet?"

"I saw her on the first day I came to school in Clarksbury. There was something that made me notice her."

"She is pretty," said Ariel.

"She is," said Peter. "But it was more than that. The way she stood apart from everyone; it was like looking in a mirror. I wanted to talk to her, but I had to pluck up a lot of courage first." He chuckled ruefully. "After a long time building up my courage, I saw these bullies picking on her. She wouldn't back down, even though she couldn't see to fight them. So, I ran in and helped her. Then I introduced myself. Then things got really strange."

Ariel looked at him. "Strange?"

"This isn't the only alien world I've visited, Ariel."

His eyes were closed, but he could picture Ariel blinking at him, so he said, "Rosemary had to go to some surreal fantasy world in order to save her brother. I went with her. I wasn't going to let her go alone."

"You followed her into a strange land to help her on a quest?" Ariel breathed. She swallowed hard. "Do you love her?"

He hesitated, then forced the truth past his lips. "Yes. I'm *in* love with her. But I don't know if she loves me."

A part of his mind spoke up, saying, of course she does, you dolt! She followed you here, didn't she?

Maybe.

Ariel slid closer and rested her head against his arm. He put his arm around her shoulder.

The clouds rolled across his mind, obscuring his thoughts.

Ariel turned back to the lake.

***

Rosemary scrambled out from under the dining room table and scampered across the floor.

Eleanna folded her arms. "Stop."

Rosemary froze, hand stuck in midair as if she were suddenly coated in glass. She couldn't even turn her head.

"Stand up," said Eleanna. "Let me see you."

The air around Rosemary pushed and prodded her until she was on her feet and facing the old woman. Her jaw strained as she tried to speak.

A smile touched Eleanna's lips. "I'm sorry. I didn't mean to frighten you."

The air binding Rosemary loosened up and rippled away. She staggered on shaky knees. She brought up her hands and glared warily at Eleanna.

"As you can see, songbreaker, some songs are harder to break than others. I may look like a frail old woman, but when I want it to be, my mind is strong." She indicated an oak chair sitting beside the dining room table. "Have a seat. Let us talk. What is your name?"

Rosemary hesitated, then decided to sit down. She crossed the floor, giving Eleanna a wide berth. She kept her eyes on Eleanna as the old woman went to the table beside her rocking chair, took a china cup, and poured some tea from a pot. She set this beside Rosemary, who stared at the brown liquid but would not drink.

Eleanna chuckled. "You can see that deception doesn't work on you, songbreaker. That is tea. Drink. It will soothe your throat."

Rosemary picked up the cup and sipped the warm liquid. She winced as her throat protested and set the cup down.

"And your name?" asked Eleanna, sitting down.

"Rosemary. Rosemary Watson."

"Did my daughter bring you here, Rosemary Watson?"

"Your daugh— Yes, I suppose you could say that."

"You've caused us quite a lot of trouble, young lady."

"Good!"

"Ah, spirit." Eleanna nodded. "Yes, you would have to have spirit in order to survive the transition between your world and ours. And you would have to be strongly linked to Peter in order to come here at all."

"You might say that, too," said Rosemary. "Well, I'm here now, and since you're obviously not going to kill me, or else you would have done so already, I'd like to know what you're going to do about it."

Eleanna didn't answer. She sipped her tea for a long moment before setting it aside.

"You've met Merius and Fionarra, my children?" she said. "The heirs to my throne once I pass on — which I will, despite Fionarra's desire to the contrary, poor girl. Tell me, Rosemary, what sort of leaders would they be?"

Rosemary didn't answer, but her raised eyebrows told the story.

Eleanna nodded. "Their rivalry is bitter and intense, as only sibling rivalries can be. If either became leader of this village, the other would not accept it. It would do great harm to the community. But then we have Peter."

Rosemary blinked. "You're going to make Peter leader instead?"

"I will not lie to you, Rosemary," said Eleanna. "I want Peter to stay. He would stay if he was truly alone, but he isn't. He has you."

"And I'm a songbreaker."

"Understand that if our village didn't need Peter, we would realize our mistake and return him to you. But we *do* need Peter. It is only your songbreaking ability that is preventing me from sending you back to your beach right now, bound in iron."

"So, what will you do?"

Eleanna got up from her rocking chair. Rosemary gripped the edge of the table, ready to fight, but the old woman didn't approach her. She studied the far corner of the room, deep in thought.

Then she turned on Rosemary. "You may make a challenge for the heart of Peter McAllister."

"Challenge? His *heart?*"

"I will give you one opportunity. I will tell no one of your visit here: not Merius, not Fionarra. Hide yourself until the Homecoming Ceremony. If you cannot break the glamour enthralling Peter at that time, then he is ours. If you can sway him to your side, he is yours."

"Why do you always refer to Peter as property?"

"However you do it, this is your only chance," said Eleanna. "If you fail, then Peter is ours, and you will leave immediately, or be killed."

"How am I going to infiltrate the Homecoming Ceremony? I don't know what the Homecoming Ceremony is!"

"It is a procession leading Peter through the village to the central square where he will drink of the chalice and be made a part of our world. He will be 'welcomed by our blood,' as the saying goes. There are dancers and an honour guard. The entire village will be there, ready to welcome our new arrival."

"Honour guard? The whole village? How can I challenge that?"

Eleanna stepped to a closet and pulled out a bundle of sea-green silk. She tossed this to Rosemary. "You will also have this."

Rosemary stared at the hem of a long dress.

"That dress is worn by members of the Welcome Circle. They surround the initiate along the parade route and dance to celebrate the Homecoming."

Rosemary goggled. "You expect me to dance?"

"No, I expect you to fail," said Eleanna. "But this is the chance that, by law, I must give you."

"How do I know I can trust you?"

"Trust or do not trust, that is your choice," said Eleanna. "But this is your only opportunity. Now go."

Silence descended upon the room. Rosemary looked from the bundle of fabric to Eleanna and back again. Eleanna said nothing. Finally, Rosemary stood up. Carrying the clothes under her arm, she made for the door.

Eleanna returned to her rocking chair. As Rosemary stepped into the hall, she called, "Good luck."

Rosemary hesitated, and then said, "Thank you." Then she was gone.

★★★

Rosemary retreated to the dead end where she'd woken up after fleeing the mob. She couldn't say why, but she felt safe there, and it seemed an appealing place for a base of operations. As she entered it, she felt like she was passing a curtain of shadow.

She examined the bundle in her hands: a loose, flowing dress with an off-the-shoulder neck, a long shawl-scarf of the same fabric, and length after length of transparent, sea-green gauze. There were no shoes. Did the dancers go barefoot? Her shoes would probably stand out unless she painted them green.

She stripped off her clothes and stuffed them at the base of the cliff. She slid on the green dress, which was only a little tight around her waist and fell to her ankles. Actually, it looked good, except for her shoulders.

She sighed at the white straps. "The bra is a dead giveaway." She undid her brassiere and hid it with the rest of her clothes. Then she placed the shawl-scarf behind her neck and wrapped the ends along both arms.

"I could wear this to the Halloween Homecoming Dance," she muttered. Then she looked at the strips of gauze. "But I have *no* idea what to do with you."

Then she froze. Voices had returned to the village.

She heard chatter in the windows and drawers being opened and closed. She heard footfalls in the gullies, and a hunting party returning to the junction closest to her hideout.

"She could be anywhere, Merius," a woman snapped. "We cannot hope to find her unless she returns to the village."

"It is rare for Fionarra and Merius to stand together on an issue," said a young man.

"It is vital that we find and neutralize the song-breaker," rumbled Merius.

"Vital, yes," said Fionarra. "But much as I wish to continue the search, we would be wasting our time. The Homecoming Ceremony must not be delayed."

This brought silence to the hunting party. Rosemary pressed herself as close as she dared to the curtain of shadow.

"Hold the ceremony as planned?" the young man spluttered. "With the songbreaker so close at hand?"

"She can't break our hold on Peter once he endures the ceremony," snapped Fionarra.

"Endures?" Rosemary mouthed.

Fionarra went on. "Delaying making Peter one of us is precisely what the songbreaker wants. Therefore, we have to act now."

"Fionarra's right," said Merius grudgingly. "When Peter is one of us, there will be no reason for the songbreaker to stay. She may even leave willingly, though I am loath to take the risk."

"Enough," snapped Fionarra. "I call for a vote."

"Fionarra," the young man gasped. "We are not in chambers —"

"Eleven of us are here; all but one of the council," Fionarra stormed. "I call for a vote!"

"Very well." The young man cleared his throat. "Those in favour of cancelling the ceremony until the songbreaker is found?"

There was a shuffle of hands. Then the chairman said, "Five. All opposed?"

Another shuffle of hands. "Five. We have a tie. As chairman, I must now cast the deciding vote, and I —"

"We do not have a tie," said Fionarra curtly. "Eleanna is not here, and as she is my mother, I hold her vote. She stands with me."

"Fionarra —"

"She is my mother too," rumbled Merius. "If she doesn't stand with Fionarra, then she stands with me, and I also vote to hold the ceremony."

The chairman sighed. "As you wish. The vote carries. Send for Peter. Tell him the ceremony is about to begin."

***

Peter listened to the surf. The sound washed over his mind, drowning his spinning thoughts. He closed his eyes and was alone in a universe of waves and his breathing. He relaxed. Unbidden, his mind reached out.

There was a sickening thump.

He fell on the ice-hardened asphalt. A pain shot up his arm.

He stumbled forward, feet slipping on the icy path, struggling for the gate and the crowd of people surrounding the scene.

"Mom! Dad!" Some in the crowd turned. Arms clasped around him, holding him back.

"There's nothing you can do, Son!"

"Stay back! The ambulance is on its way!"

"No!" Peter squealed. "Mom!"

A policeman grabbed him. Peter tried to beat him back. The pain from his broken arm blackened his sight. The next thing he remembered, he was sitting in a wheelchair, his arm in a cast, a doctor leaning close. Behind him, at the other end of the waiting area, sliding doors parted and paramedics pushed a gurney through.

"Peter?" The doctor tried again. "Peter, we've contacted your uncle. He's coming back from London on the next available flight, but he won't be here until tomorrow."

Peter stared vacantly ahead.

The doctor sucked his lip. He looked over his shoulder. "He's not responsive."

A woman leaned in, her smile a coax. "Peter? I'm Jane Richards from Children's Services. Doug Petersen's my partner. We'll find you a place to stay tonight, until your uncle can see you."

Peter said nothing.

Jane frowned at her colleague. He could only shrug. She turned back. "Peter, do you know if your parents had a will or signed some document that said who would take care of you when your mom and dad ... weren't around?"

Peter looked away.

"Surely it doesn't matter," said the doctor. "The boy has an uncle!"

"But no sign of a will," said Jane. "From what I've heard, his uncle is away on business six months out of the year. The rules clearly state who has to care for the child in this case."

The doctor glanced at Peter and pulled the social workers back. Not far enough, however; Peter could still hear them.

"The boy's lost his parents, for God's sake. The last thing he needs is to be shuffled from foster home to foster home. When his uncle gets here, he should get custody immediately!"

"I have to work within the law, doctor," Jane snapped. "Look, I promise you that Peter will get the best care possible until we can work out this tragic situation. I promise!"

Peter opened his eyes. Across the hospital waiting room, he saw Fiona, short-haired, distraught, and human, talking with two police officers. One of the officers pointed at Peter. Fiona nodded, and they turned and left.

She took a step towards him, and stopped, her eyes fixed on his vacant stare. She looked at him a long time across the hospital room as people passed before her and behind. Then her gaze lowered to the floor.

She turned and slipped into the flow of people. The hospital doors slid shut behind her, cutting her from Peter's view.

The conversations blurred and rushed back into the sounds of the surf. Peter blinked at the water. His cheeks were wet again.

He scrambled to his feet and looked at the world as though he was seeing it for the first time. Ariel stared at him. "Peter?"

He clambered off the rock, slipped, and fell on the stones. He pushed himself to his feet.

Ariel slipped off the rock. "Peter!"

Across the stony beach, people were running to him. Fiona was in the lead, her red hair flowing behind her like a torch. She stopped lightly before him and clasped his hands. "Peter!" she breathed. "It's time."

"Who are you?" Peter mumbled. "Why did you bring me here?"

A look of horror flashed across Fiona's face. It blew a shot of clarity into his mind. This was wrong. She was an impostor. He wasn't supposed to be here.

But the next instant, Fiona hid her look of horror. She smiled at Peter, her eyes narrowed, and she flicked her hair over her shoulder. He could feel the veil being pulled over his consciousness.

"No!" He struggled. "I'm not supposed to be —"

She wrapped her arms around him and kissed him. His eyes grew glassy. His hands moved of their own accord to embrace her. Peter could see himself as though his mind had been pulled from his body, and cast out to sea. The waves of Fiona's smell and her beauty washed over him, swamping him. He struggled to stay afloat.

Fiona pulled away. "Are you ready?" she asked.

"Yes." The voice was not his.

The other villagers gathered around him, positioning themselves in front of Peter and Ariel. A group of musicians holding bodhrans and primitive stringed instruments started to play a slow, rhythmic processional. The sirens began a wailing chant. Surrounded by the honour guard, Peter and Ariel walked back towards the village.

Peter's consciousness floated out to sea.

Chapter Thirteen
Initiation

Rosemary peered from behind a stone column at the edge of the siren caves and spotted a group of twelve ethereal sea-women, dressed in Welcome Circle finery, huddled and chattering on the path leading back to the bay. Some were practising their dance steps. Rosemary cast a critical eye at their flowing robes and veils, and looked down at herself. She slipped back into the shadows and adjusted her own clothing, peering out to check that she was dressed properly.

She took note of their feet and huffed. "They *would* be barefoot." She shucked her shoes.

Finally, she felt ready; scarves covered her finless pink arms, and her skirts billowed in the breeze. With the veil concealing her face below the eyes, it was an effective disguise, but Rosemary decided she didn't want to chance being recognized until she absolutely had to. So she stayed in hiding, peering out to watch the Welcome Circle wait and practise.

She frowned as she followed the movement of their feet. "Wait a minute," she muttered. She mimicked the steps. Heel-toe, heel-toe. "I know these steps!" Heel-toe, twist. "That's step-dancing!"

The moves had been modified, danced at half-speed with added arm gestures, but they were still recognizable to the girl who'd spent an agonizing summer jumping in Irish clod-shoes, arms pressed to her sides.

"Scavengers," she muttered, shaking her head. Or survivors, she thought, remembering Merius and his "Lost Children" speech. How many of these, she wondered, could trace their history to the shipwrecks in that transitional world? Lots, she thought.

But there hadn't been a shipwreck on the Bruce Peninsula for decades.

How old *are* these people?

Then she heard drumbeats in the distance and looked up. An honour guard was approaching from the bay, wailing, beating drums, and playing a variety of stringed instruments. As the procession drew nearer, the women of the Welcome Circle stopped chattering and organized themselves into a line. Rosemary waited and, when the women moved out at a silent cue, she darted out of the shadows and brought up the rear.

As she danced after the Welcome Circle, she glanced up and almost stumbled. Leading the honour guard was Fionarra. Rosemary brought up an arm to hide her face, but Fionarra's gaze was locked on the parade route. Rosemary was by her in a second, and circling Peter from ten feet away. He was flanked by a young siren and surrounded by marchers. Too many people, Rosemary thought. No room even for a mad dash.

Before she had a chance to plan, the Welcome Circle surrounded Peter, raising their arms in the air and twirling once. Rosemary barely kept up the movement.

"Just remember your classes," she muttered beneath her breath. "Heel-toe, heel-toe, twist."

The steps weren't intricate; nor did the women match each other exactly, which was fortunate. After a minute, Rosemary moved with more confidence, and kept her gaze on Peter and the crowd.

As the procession wound its way among the stone pillars, sirens emerged from their homes, standing on their turf-covered roofs to cheer Peter. The air shuddered with their cries. Rosemary didn't see the sirens climbing the rock faces; she only saw them emerge from their caves, or standing above them. She felt like she was in a canyon, sirens lining the rim.

There were at least two people marching between her and Peter at any given moment. Still no opportunity. She scowled beneath her veil as she mimicked the Welcome Circle's hand gestures.

She wondered where Merius was. Then she saw him take up a place along the route, clenching his trident and watching the parade with a critical eye. Rosemary lowered her eyes and tried to will herself invisible.

Then something pulled Merius's gaze from the revellers. She looked ahead and saw Fionarra glaring at him from the head of the honour guard. The two remained focussed on each other until Rosemary was safely past.

The procession wound through the siren village until it doubled back on itself, finally emerging onto the open patch of green. In the middle, built on top of a stone depression, was a wooden stage. The park was lined with celebrants standing in eager but respectful silence. Rosemary wondered where all these people had been less than an hour ago.

The stage was five feet high and ten feet across. A set of stairs led up to it, guarded by two male sirens. They crossed their tridents as the procession approached. The musicians leading the procession turned away and joined the crowd. The Welcome Circle parted and slipped around the stage like the tide around an island.

Peter and the siren girl walked up to the guards, and the tridents parted. The two mounted the steps alone.

The Welcome Circle twirled one last time and stopped with the music. They stood with arms upstretched, facing the stage.

The people who had lined the parade route filed into the square, filling the remaining spaces. Rosemary saw Merius standing near the entrance, trident in hand, casting a wary eye over his shoulder and then across the crowd.

For several minutes, everyone in the square stood still. The siren girl stood ramrod straight. Peter stared glassily ahead. As she stood in silence with arms over her head, Rosemary knew she'd be getting a cramp soon. It had to be dancing, she thought. For once, why can't I disrupt a ceremony with algebra?

Finally, Fionarra handed her trident to an attendant and mounted the steps to the raised dais at the head of the square. She faced Peter over the crowd.

Her soft voice carried easily across the silent multitude. "Council, villagers: we welcome to our family one Peter McAllister. Lost for years, we have now found him. Away from us, he has come home. By these words and by our blood, we make Peter one of us, and ...," she looked at Peter and allowed herself a small smile, "... welcome him into our hearts."

She glanced down. "Give Ariel the chalice."

The siren girl turned and accepted a pitcher and a chalice from someone in the crowd. The pitcher was cut crystal, and the golden chalice looked as if it belonged in a church — and, thought Rosemary, it probably did. Ariel set these between herself and Peter and poured out water from the pitcher.

Rosemary shifted on her feet. Time was running out, but the guards still stood at the steps. The stage in front of her would not be an easy climb, but it looked as though she was going to have to chance it.

Ariel reached to the crowd. Someone handed her a trident and she turned back to Peter, holding the weapon between them, points in the air. He hesitated, but grabbed hold of the staff. Ariel smiled and nodded. Then she stepped back and flexed her arm. She took a deep breath, and then swung down her hand, slamming her palm on the centre point of the trident.

Rosemary flinched. The long sleeves of her robes slipped and bunched up at her shoulders.

The crowd stayed silent as Ariel pulled her hand back and held it, palm open, over the chalice. Blood welled from the cut and dripped into the water until the water was tinged red.

Finally, Ariel wrapped a piece of her robe around her palm and took up the chalice. She came close to Peter and held the cup between them.

Fionarra drew herself up. "Peter Calvin McAllister, do you come here of your own free will?"

Peter bowed his head. He barely blinked. "I do."

"Do you wish to join our family?"

"No," breathed Rosemary.

Again, Peter nodded. "I do."

Fionarra's smile widened. "Do you consent to become like us?"

"Say no," Rosemary whispered.

"I do."

Rosemary clenched her teeth.

"Peter Calvin McAllister." Fionarra's voice echoed across the square. "We welcome you. Before you drink of the chalice, answer this: do you know of any ties that bind you to another world and keep you from joining our family?"

Rosemary fixed her eyes on Peter. "Say yes," she whispered. "Please, say yes."

Peter opened his mouth, but no words came out. He closed it again, blinking. The silence stretched. Whispers rustled through the crowd.

Fionarra cleared her throat. "Peter?" Her eyes bore into him across the square.

Peter opened his mouth again. Then he looked around at the crowd. His gaze fell on Rosemary.

As Rosemary stood in the Welcome Circle — her arms stretched over her head — she realized that with her sleeves bunched around her shoulders, her arms were bare. The bloody bandage over the bite on her forearm was plain for all to see, and Peter was looking directly at it. Then his gaze flickered from her bandage to her eyes. The glassiness vanished from his eyes. Recognition lit his face.

Fionarra followed Peter's gaze to Rosemary, and she let out a howl of anger that made the air quake. She leapt forward, pointing.

"Stop her! It's the songbreaker!"

The crowd screamed, roared and ran in several directions at once.

Rosemary dropped her arms and charged the stage.

The guards at the steps brought their tridents to bear. Without thinking, Rosemary grabbed the shaft of one to pull it aside, but the moment she touched the metal, the guard disappeared. The trident clattered to the ground.

More screams echoed through the square.

Rosemary bit her lip as she stared at the ground where the guard had been, but she picked up the trident and, in a flash of inspiration, held up her right hand at the remaining guard, palm open, revealing the birthmark. "Stand aside, unless you want to be broken too!"

Please, she added to herself.

The guard dropped to his knees and cowered.

Rosemary clambered up the steps.

To her left and her right, she saw five guards rushing through the crowd, pushing past people with unnatural ease, tridents ready, their faces grim. Behind her, she could hear Merius yelling furiously. Fionarra was running at the stage, unarmed, her rage darkening the air. These, Rosemary sensed, wouldn't be scared off by strong words and a birthmark.

A trident's staff smashed into her shins. She fell; her own weapon went sliding. Panicked, she scrambled to her feet. Peter and Ariel stood in front of her, staring. Rosemary knocked the chalice out of the girl's hands, shouldered her aside, and grabbed Peter by the back of the neck.

He blinked at her. "Rosemary?"

Glamour. What had Merius told her? "*You can break glamour for a few seconds, through some shock like cold water, a kiss, or a firebrand.*" She didn't have the water, and she didn't want to burn him.

But this all started with a ... "Peter!" she shouted, and kissed him.

For a moment, the noise of the crowd faded as his lips softened under hers. Then the cries came back into focus. Rosemary could hear Fionarra yelling, "Seize her!" like some made-up villain.

Rosemary released the kiss, leaving Peter gasping for air. She looked him in the eye. Peter looked back. "Peter?"

"Rosemary? What are you ...?" His face fell open as he looked around. "What the ... where am I?"

"You're awake, that's all that matters," said Rosemary. She could hear footfalls rushing the stage. "We've got to run."

She pulled at him, but he didn't move. His face was closing. He wasn't even looking at her anymore.

"*Unless blocked by an exceptionally strong mind, glamour simply reasserts itself.*" Great, she told herself, way to remember only half your instructions. Peter had been here too long. They could have done anything to weaken his defences. She could feel the glamour building up on him like ice. She shook his shoulders. "Peter! No, wake up!"

"Rosemary," he breathed. "You shouldn't be here."

"Peter!" she shouted. She snapped her fingers in front of his face, slapped him. "No, no, no! Peter, you've got to wake up! Wake up!"

She lunged to kiss him again, but Merius grabbed her from behind and threw her off the stage. She landed heavily in the arms of two other sirens, who shoved her to the ground and held her there.

Rosemary looked up. Peter stared glassily ahead. The little siren girl was sitting on the stage, bewildered. Fionarra was frantically gathering up the pitcher and chalice. Rosemary struggled to sit up, but the sirens — it was the two from the beach, Loria and Darius — pushed her down.

"You have failed," said Eleanna, looming over her

like a standing stone. "You will leave now, Rosemary Watson, or be killed."

"No!" Rosemary shouted. "You didn't give him a chance! I'm not leaving him here!"

"Then you choose death," said Eleanna.

Rosemary struggled, shouting every obscenity she knew. She broke free and clawed her way along the ground towards the stage. She looked up and saw Peter staring back, stiff as a mannequin. "Peter!" she screamed. "Wake up!"

Then the sirens grabbed her, rolled her on her back, pinned her against the stage. Merius strode forward, his trident raised to strike.

And then Rosemary just screamed.

Then she heard a voice scream, "Stop!"

Peter stumbled into her view, a trident in his hands. He stood over her, waving the weapon wildly. "Stop it! Stop it!"

Silence fell. Everyone stood tense. The only sound through the crowd of sirens was Rosemary and Peter's ragged breathing.

"Peter," Eleanna intoned. "This is our business. Don't interfere."

"No," said Peter, shaking his head as he fought to clear it. "No, this is wrong. You keep trying to hurt Rosemary! My family would never do that!"

Fionarra raised her hands. "Peter, please —"

He brought up a hand to shield his eyes. "Just stop! You did something to me! I can't think straight whenever I look at you. None of this feels right!" The air shimmered to his words.

Fionarra swallowed. "P-peter —"

"Shut up, Fiona, wait! You said ... you said you had to search for me when you heard my parents died," said Peter. "But ... you were there! You were at the hospital, but you wouldn't speak to me. Either you *could* have rescued me then and didn't, or that wasn't you!"

"Peter, please," said Eleanna. "Let us explain."

"No!" Peter yelled, swinging the trident around as Merius got too close. "You lied to bring me here! I don't belong here! Stop telling me lies!"

His voice echoed. The air shimmered like a tuning fork. People vanished or merged together. Walls and ceilings turned to dust and the wind whistled through the desolation. Where one hundred and fifty-seven sirens once stood, only thirteen remained.

Peter stared, the trident loose in his hands. The remaining sirens stood about, arms at their sides, looking embarrassed, as though they suddenly found themselves naked.

"You don't even look like me," Peter breathed.

Then Fionarra swooped past, knocking Peter off his feet. His trident went flying. She pinned him down and snarled, her triangular teeth inches from his face. Peter's eyes were wide.

"Peter!" Rosemary reached for him, struggled to get up, but Merius shoved her back.

"You have reduced us to the real, songbreaker," he said. "You have nothing left to threaten us with."

Rosemary could only watch as Fionarra raised a clawed hand to strike.

"That's enough!" Ariel grabbed Fionarra's arm. The little girl pulled back, hard, and Rosemary heard a crack. Fionarra's arm bent in a direction it wasn't supposed to go and she rocked back, gasping.

But more than the arm had broken. The air around Fionarra's arm had cracked too, and the cracks were spreading, onto the stage, through the ground beneath Rosemary, throughout the square, into other sirens. They webbed the sky like glass. Sirens shouted, turned to run, but were caught.

The world shattered and came raining down. The stage disappeared, sending Rosemary sprawling. Particles pattered around her, vanishing in puffs of smoke. The ruined walls crumbled, as did the trees and the ground, until nothing was left. Rosemary found herself on her back, looking up into fog.

She sat up. Peter, sprawled beside her, lifted his head. They were back in their old clothes, on a stony beach beside a big rock. The cliff rose behind them and the water lapped at their feet. Waves rumbled in the distance and the wind whistled, but beyond a ten-foot radius, fog shrouded everything like the end of the world.

Their eyes fell on the only siren left standing.

Ariel buried her face in her hands.

Rosemary shook her head. "Was *any* of it real?"

Ariel looked up, then turned away. "Memories are real. This place echoes its memories: the shipwrecks, the nightmares of drowned children, the survivors. I remembered the people of my village. In the end, it was all I had left."

Peter and Rosemary helped each other to their feet. The waves crashed. The silence stretched.

"So ...," said Peter slowly. "When Fiona came to me, told me about this place ... that was you?"

"A part of me," Ariel whispered. "I made Fionarra for your benefit, Peter, so I could tempt you here and give you other reasons to stay."

"How?" Peter stammered. "How did you know —"

"I looked into your mind," said Ariel. "I saw the moment that made you so like me. I took the one element from that memory that I could use to talk to you."

"Fiona," breathed Peter. "Because she was the only one alive."

Rosemary bit her lip.

"I altered my world to make Fionarra fit," said Ariel. "It wasn't always comfortable. She came into conflict with my memory of Merius, but it worked. Fionarra was for your benefit, but the rest ... the rest was for me. Even Eleanna, who taught me how to use glamour. All were as I remembered them."

Peter goggled. "Why did you do this?"

"Because I'm alone." Ariel cleared her nose with a sniff. "I had parents long ago, and friends, before the sirens took me in. With their help, I learnt to make my own family, who took care of me, loved me, argued with me, and have been everything to me. Through it all I knew that I'd lost so much that was real. I had to find someone to share my loneliness with. Someone who understood."

Rosemary opened her mouth, but Ariel spoke first. "Yes, I was human, once. My parents drowned. I had a life jacket. And that was how the sirens found me and brought me here, a Lost Child."

"What happened to everyone?" asked Rosemary.

"They grew old and died, grew sick and died, or just disappeared," said Ariel. "After me, the Lost Ones stopped coming. The villagers didn't see their doom until it was too late. They had been building sandcastles for so long, they did not notice the tide had come in."

Rosemary stepped to Ariel's side, turned her around, and crouched low. "I-I'm ... so sorry."

Ariel drew herself up. "No. *I* am sorry. I took something that did not belong to me. Promise me you'll never forget how lucky you are that you have each other."

Rosemary gave her a small smile. "I promise. What will you do now?"

"Rebuild my world. Perhaps someone else will come along and I can share it."

"No, wait a minute, wait a minute!" Peter strode forward. "I know I don't belong here, but what about you? You're human!"

Ariel shook her head. "Only in memory."

"That's not true!" He grabbed her wrist. "Come with us! We can look for your relatives. We can put you among your own people. You can find friends, rebuild your life, we —"

"Peter, you don't understand." She shook herself free and displayed her arm, showing sea-glass skin and a fin growing on the back of it. "I've been through the Homecoming Ceremony. I'm not human anymore ... and I'm older than you think. This world may be dead, but my world died a long time ago."

Peter shook his head. "No. There has to be a way —"

"There is no way!" Ariel yelled. She continued more softly. "Your world is your true home, and this world is mine. Goodbye." She hugged Peter, hard, and then stepped back. The wind picked up, plucking at her hair and tattered robes. She faded into streamers of mist, until empty air remained.

Peter turned away.

Rosemary stumbled forward. "Wait! What about us? How do we get out of here?"

Ariel's voice echoed over the waves. "You have broken most of this world's glamour, songbreaker, but one piece remains. It holds you here now. Break it, and you can return home, and we can start to rebuild. You already know how."

Then the only sound was the wind and the waves.

Rosemary turned to Peter. He stood looking at the spot where Ariel had stood, as though at a gravestone. The wind blew the minutes away. Finally, she touched his shoulder.

He turned to her. His cheeks were wet.

She opened her mouth to say something, then hesitated. Reaching up, she wiped his tears away. Then she clasped his shoulder.

"It ends with a kiss," she said.

He frowned a moment before he understood. He cleared his nose with a sniff, then he straightened up. He put a hand on her side, and smiled nervously. They edged closer. They wrapped their arms around each other. Rosemary looked into Peter's eyes and leaned into him. After a brief hesitation, they pressed their lips together.

The world shuddered around them and water splashed over them. They were submerged. They slipped apart in shock.

Lungs burning, Rosemary struck out, kicking for where instinct told her the surface was. She rose through foot after foot of murky water, fighting to hold her breath as the light brightened.

She burst into the air with a hacking gasp.

"Peter!" she screamed. "Pete—"

She struggled to look for the shore, but she was almost blind. A wave rolled over her. She flailed like a drowning man.

Peter grabbed her from behind and held her head above water. "I've got you!"

The foghorn of Cape Croker's lighthouse moaned. The fog rolled back. Sunlight touched the water's surface. The shoreline pulled closer. Two figures ran up the beach towards them.

Then they felt stones beneath their feet and Peter and Rosemary stood up, dripping. The wind broke against their backs. Benson ran into the water while Veronica stood, hands over her mouth, white as a sheet.

"Are you guys okay?" Benson grabbed their arms and pulled them ashore. "What happened?"

Shivering and gasping, Peter and Rosemary looked at each other. Their jeans were black with water. Rosemary's cardigan was as matted as a soaked sheep. Their hair clung to their cheeks. Rosemary's glasses were gone, but a look passed between them. She smiled. "It wasn't a dream." Despite the cold, Peter found himself smiling back.

"What are you grinning about?" said Benson. "You almost died!"

Veronica was shaking worse than they were. "You're okay," she sobbed. "It's a miracle!"

"Come on," said Benson. "If we don't get you into dry clothes, you'll freeze. C'mon, you two, let's go home, okay?"

"Home," said Peter. Rosemary took his hand and squeezed it. "Yeah. I'm home."

Clutching each other, they stumbled up the stony beach towards Clarksbury.

Chapter Fourteen
Homecoming

Peter trudged up the country road towards Rosemary's house, his feet crunching on the gravel shoulder. He hesitated at her mailbox, staring up at her cozy home with its battered white siding. A light was on in her bedroom and he smiled at the thought of her there.

He pushed up the front walk, past a guttering jack-o-lantern and a bedsheet billowing from the branch of a tree. He pulled the doorknocker.

He was wearing dark pants and a sports jacket over a dark blue shirt. He cocked his fedora, then took it off and held it in both hands as the door opened. He stared in amazement.

Rosemary was wearing a low-cut green dress, with the sleeves pushed down her shoulders, and a long, flowing skirt. A green scarf was wrapped over her neck and arms while white scarves were draped over her shoulders in an attempt to duplicate the dress she'd worn at the Homecoming Ceremony. The attempt worked, despite the woolly fringes on the green scarf. A hint of green makeup shadowed her eyes. The sequins glittered in the twilight.

"Hi!" she said, smiling.

"Wow ...." He cut himself off. "I mean ... hi! Hi, Rosemary! You look ... great!"

Rosemary snickered. "I'm glad you like it. Everybody else will think I'm going as a green vampire, but who cares? What are you supposed to be?"

"A journalist, see?" He held out his hat, showing her an index card he'd placed on the brim with the word "PRESS" written on it in felt-tip pen.

Rosemary raised her eyebrows.

He grinned sheepishly. "All I had was my uncle's wardrobe. It was either this or a stockbroker."

The front door opened and Mr. Watson poked his head out. "Ah, hello Peter! You're ready to go, I see. I'll drive you two over as soon as I finish setting up the display."

From behind him, they heard Trish's voice. "Are those trick-or-treaters at our door?"

He popped back inside, leaving Peter and Rosemary to stand in nervous silence.

"Trish is handling the trick-or-treaters," said

Rosemary, grinning. "She's really excited. It's usually my job."

Peter shifted on his feet. "So, what did you tell your folks ... about us?"

"Not much," she replied. "I said I'd cornered you at the beach, and that we talked, and that as we talked, a big wave rolled in and soaked us both. So long as Benson and Veronica keep quiet about our run up the cliff, there's nothing else they need to know."

"Wouldn't they understand?"

"They'd understand, but I don't think they'd like it if they thought I was making a habit of visiting crazy worlds. You?"

"My uncle doesn't know a thing."

"You two don't talk much, do you?"

"I'll try," said Peter. "I promise. He's ...." He sucked his lip. "He's the one family member I've got left."

Rosemary clasped his hands. "I know it's hard." Then she faltered. "Actually, I don't. I've never ... but ... you know what I mean?"

"Yeah." He smiled at her. "Ariel really knew how to get at me. She may have come for me looking like my old babysitter, but it's when she gave me a sister that I most wanted to stay. It was a dirty trick. But I know how *she* feels. She was like me in a way. I wish we hadn't left her behind."

"You're *not* like her, you know," said Rosemary. "She didn't have anything. You do. Not just your uncle. You've got friends."

He looked away. "I'm realizing that now."

"And ... if you want parents, you can borrow mine."

He looked at her. "Really?"

Rosemary blushed in the twilight and couldn't meet his eyes.

His mouth dried up and his heart began to thump. "Rosemary, I ...." She looked at him expectantly.

A scream cut through the air.

A witch with glowing eyes popped out of the garden and bobbed menacingly on a string.

Rosemary and Peter looked at it, then at each other, and burst out laughing.

Mr. Watson stepped out of the garage. "Well, what did you think?" His face fell at the sight of Peter and Rosemary, bent double with laughter. "Not the effect I was going for."

* * *

Rosemary's father drove them through Clarksbury's downtown. Chattering students in costume walked along the sidewalks. Then the car turned right instead of left.

"Wait a minute," said Peter. "Isn't the dance at the school?"

224

Rosemary raised an eyebrow. "Who didn't read the posters?"

"I didn't think I was going to the dance!"

"You'll start reading those posters now, won't you, Peter?" Mr. Watson cut in.

He chuckled as the two blushed.

They pulled up to the marina. A stony beach stretched away past the breakwater. A miniature lighthouse flashed red at the edge of a pier. The arms of the Niagara Escarpment reached into Georgian Bay, glowing red in the setting sun. A crowd mingled on a wooden patio and the beach. The crackle of the bonfire and the beat of the music echoed across the rolling water.

Peter stared.

Rosemary nudged him. "Why do you think I'm wearing sneakers in this dress?"

He laughed. "You couldn't be more of a siren than you are now."

She slugged him in the shoulder, playfully.

"Rosemary!" Veronica called, dressed as a witch in running shoes. She stopped short at Rosemary's costume. "Wow!"

"Hey, Rosemary!" Joe crunched across the stones to them. "You brought him over! Cool!"

"He didn't kick or scream at all," said Rosemary. "I was almost disappointed."

Peter nodded to his captain. "Thanks for having me, Joe."

"You're always welcome." He waved them towards the patio. "The dance is just starting."

They stepped onto the deck and planted themselves by the railing.

Veronica stepped forward and grabbed Benson by the elbow. "Hey, Benson."

He blinked at her. "What?"

"Come on!" She pulled him to the dance floor. He followed, looking bewildered. Grinning, Joe sauntered out after them and danced with everyone.

Rosemary and Peter stood by the railing, staring like wallflowers.

Peter leaned close to her ear. "So ... what do we do now?"

She stared at the shaking bodies, and raised her hands. "Um ... I guess we ... dance."

He took a deep breath. "Okay!" He pushed away from the railing.

She yanked him back. "Not now! I can't dance to that, that's a fast song!"

He stared at her. "So ... what, we just stand here?"

The fast music eased and the Tori Amos song, "One Thousand Oceans," started playing through the speakers. The dance floor thinned out, but couples stayed behind to clasp each other close and rock in slow circles.

Rosemary gripped Peter's arm. "Now," she said. Her knuckles whitened.

He swallowed hard. "Okay."

They found a space amid the couples and faced each other. Each tried to put their arms around the other, but gave up awkwardly. Then Peter grabbed Rosemary's arms, flung them behind him, and pulled her close. "There. That wasn't so hard, was it?"

"Mmph," said Rosemary.

"Sorry." He loosened his grip.

They shuffled in a small circle to the music. Rosemary bit her lip. Peter's face clouded with fear, but neither turned away.

"Rosemary ...." He took a deep breath. "I ... I think I love you."

Her mouth quirked. "I think you do, too."

They laughed at that. The tension eased from their shoulders.

Then Rosemary's smile faded, and she looked him in the eye. "I love you, too, Peter."

Their faces drew closer and their lips met. And it was the most right thing in the world.

END